I0716911

TRICKSTER

COVEN: BOOK 8

DAVID NETH

DN Publishing

Trickster
Coven, Book 8
Copyright © 2022 by David Neth
Batavia, NY

www.DavidNethBooks.com

ISBN: 978-1-945336-26-3
First Edition

Subscribe to the author's newsletter for updates and exclusive content:
DavidNethBooks.com/Newsletter

Follow the author at:
www.facebook.com/DavidNethBooks

Also by David Neth

<u>Coven</u>
Harpy
Siren
Valkyrie
Shapeshifter
Sorcerer
Witch (Short Story)
Enchantress
Oracle
Trickster
Poltergeist
Hex (Short Story)
Witch Hunter

<u>Under the Moon</u>
The Full Moon
The Harvest Moon
The Blood Moon
The Crescent Moon
The Blue Moon

The Art of Magic

<u>Fuse</u>
Origin
Omertá
Oblivion

<u>Heat</u>
Black Magnet
Dust Storm
The Gatekeeper

<u>Standalone</u>
All I Ever Wanted

CHAPTER 1

- MAY 1989 -

Samantha felt the tears well up in her eyes. Her breath shuddered and her chest heaved.

This was her worst nightmare.

"So you've been lying to me?" Steven asked at the foot of the stairs.

"I was trying to make you feel included." She stood in the foyer, her meager attempt to keep him from leaving.

"By keeping a secret from me?" He turned and started up the stairs.

She raced after him and tugged on his arm. The two of them stopped halfway up the stairs. "I didn't want you to feel alone or left out because you were the only one who wasn't a witch."

"Look around, Sam! I'm the only man in this house too and

somehow I manage!" He pulled his hand away from hers and continued up the stairs. "You should've been honest with me."

"I didn't want you to have to worry about our child having magic and being in danger. I didn't want to put that pressure on you, like you have with me." She followed him right into their bedroom.

Steven pulled open the closet and dug out the suitcase from the back. "But I still would be worried once they came. You just didn't want me to know about it. It'd be like you keeping the whole pregnancy from me. It's *purposely* deceitful and I just can't see past that."

"I wasn't trying to deceive you." She looked down at the suitcase open on the bed. Then, as Steven opened his dresser and started tossing his clothes in, she asked in a panicked voice, "What are you doing? Why are you packing?"

"I'm leaving, Samantha."

She came around the bed, getting between him and the suitcase. "No! We can talk about this! I'm sorry! I'm so sorry!" Tears ran down her cheeks as her voice grew more hysterical.

"It's a little too late for that, Sam." He stepped around her and dumped another drawer of clothes in the suitcase. He wasn't stopping to fold or sort anything. Clearly, he wanted to get out of there as soon as possible. "If you lied about this, how do I know you're not lying about something else? Or will again when the kid actually comes?"

"Please." Her voice strained and she felt her knees go weak.

She clutched on to him, another desperate attempt to change the outcome. "Please don't go. This was all a mistake. I didn't mean for this—I didn't think you'd be this hurt by this!"

"Well, then, you shouldn't have lied."

She clung to his arm, trying to hug him, but also trying to stop him from packing. If he would just look at her, maybe then he would agree to stay. "Let's just take a moment to cool down. Talk about this later after we've had some time to think. Steven, I love you."

For the first time, he met her eyes. What she saw wasn't love or compassion. It was pain, mixed with anger and, if she was being honest with herself, a hint of disgust.

She found herself repulsive. How could she do this to him? To their marriage?

"I need to go." He zipped his suitcase, which surprisingly he didn't have any trouble closing up. Using two hands, he took ahold of the handles and hauled it to the door and down the stairs.

Samantha was on his tail, following behind. "Can you at least give me the number of where you're staying? Maybe we can talk tonight after a little bit."

"I don't know where I'm going, exactly. I just know I need to go." He stood by the front door and fished for his keys on the table.

Samantha spotted them first and reached for them, clutching them to her chest so he couldn't leave.

"Give me my keys, Sam."

"No," she said firmly. "You're not going. This isn't—let's talk. We can fix this!"

"No, we can't. There's nothing to talk about. You made the decision for me when you lied about our child. And now you continue to try to control me by keeping me here. This is it. This is the final straw. We're done."

Samantha let out a sob and felt her knees weaken at his words. "No!"

Steven held out his hand, the other on his suitcase. His face was stoic. She searched it for any regret. Any pain. Any sense of loss that their marriage was over.

Nothing.

Slowly, she gave in and handed him his keys. He walked through the front door without a goodbye. She stood on the porch and watched as he wheeled the suitcase to his car, tossed it in the trunk, then drove off.

CHAPTER 2

The brakes hissed on the train as it came to its stopping point at Erie Forge and Steel. Alex Trillanski approached one of the cars and pulled open the sliding metal door, a cigarette hanging out of his mouth.

He'd been smoking a lot more lately. Nearly two packs a day. He'd never been under this much stress before. He wasn't sleeping, his meals were usually interrupted, and he knew from his doctor that he wasn't drinking nearly enough water. The smoking didn't help his health, but it sure did help him relax.

Hopping up into the cargo car, Alex began passing crates out the door to his coworkers, who lined up to pile them on the trucks and carry them inside. George, who started at F&S the same year as Alex, jumped up in the car with him to move the cargo out faster. The quicker they could get the train unloaded, the quicker they could get started on their work, and the quicker they could go home.

"How's your boy doing?" George asked as Alex passed another crate to someone outside the train. "Still getting over that bug?"

"Last night was terrible. Up every hour. Puking his guts out. You know how many loads of laundry I did during the hours when a man's supposed to be sleeping? Jeez, if I wasn't switching the sheets, I was getting him a glass of water, or trying to rock him back to sleep. I just hope I haven't caught it from him." He flicked the ashes from the tip of his cigarette, then stuck it back in the corner of his mouth to reach for another crate.

"Feeling any tickle in your throat?"

"Not yet, but I'll tell ya, if I keep having my sleep interrupted like this, it won't be long before I'm out too."

"Is the missus still working nights?"

Alex grunted as he lifted a particularly heavy crate. "Damn right. And after the shit she deals with over at the prison, she deserves a break too."

Irene was a security guard at the county prison. She had signed up for nights thinking that it would be perfect so she and Alex didn't have to pay for child care. Someone would always be home. Too bad the wonky schedules were kicking their butts.

"I'll bet," George said. "Wouldn't want that job, no matter how much they're paying."

"She's making decent money," Alex admitted. "But we have that credit card debt still."

"Those things'll do ya in."

Alex took a final drag of his cigarette and then flicked the butt out the door into the stone near the tracks. He looked around the train car. It was mostly empty. The remaining crates were marked for another location. Except the one in the corner. That had no labels on it.

"You know what the deal is with this one?" he asked George.

"Not sure. Probably not even ours."

Alex stepped forward to inspect the metal crate closer. "There's some weird markings on it. Looks almost…satanic or some shit."

George approached, wiping the sweat from his brow with the sleeve of his shirt. "Probably just graffiti from some kids who snuck on the train at night. Let's open it up, see if we can't figure out where it's going."

Unlike the wooden crates that had been pinned shut with thin metal staples, this crate had its own lever system to lock the doors. Alex grabbed the handle and tried to twist it open. It wouldn't budge at first and he grunted with the effort.

George grabbed ahold of another prong on the lever and helped. With the two of them, they managed to loosen it enough so that it spun freely.

"Damn, that was tight," Alex muttered.

George snickered behind him, but stopped when his

coworker pulled the door open and a large plume of black smoke erupted in their faces, sending both men falling backward on their butts in the train car.

"What the hell was that!" George gasped as the black cloud flew out of the train car and disappeared into the early morning sky.

"No idea," Alex muttered. He looked over at George. "You okay, man?"

George didn't answer. His eyes were locked on the inside of the metal crate. Slowly, he raised his hand, which was shaking with fear, and pointed inside.

Alex peered around the door of the crate and his jaw dropped.

The crate was completely empty. The only sign that it had once contained something were the deep scratches all over the metal inside. Whatever they had released was not something to be messed with.

CHAPTER 3

This one is cute!" Kathy held up a pink flowing top that she had picked from the clothing rack.

Samantha made a face. "How often do you see me wearing pink?"

"Well, you're going to be a mom. Possibly to a little girl. A lot of pink might be in your near future."

"That doesn't mean I need to get a jump start on it," Samantha said. "Besides, I'm looking for maternity *pants*. Preferably something that doesn't make me *look* pregnant."

Samantha was only three months pregnant and yet her growing belly was already making it difficult to fit into her pants. She feared what her body might look like at the end of the pregnancy. Last week, Kathy suggested that there might be twins but Samantha's stone cold glare shut that idea down real fast. Besides, her last sonogram confirmed that there was only one baby. He or she just happened to be demanding a lot of Samantha's body. Luckily, though, she had't experienced any morning sickness so far. She hoped it stayed that way. That didn't mean she hadn't been nauseated nearly every day. She just hadn't gotten sick from it.

"You're going to have to embrace it sometime." Kathy sifted through another rack of clothes. "You're only going to get bigger."

"I know, but in the meantime, I need something cute to wear to Laurel's party tomorrow." Samantha browsed through the next rack over. "Something that looks good and that I feel good in."

"Keep in mind, the party tomorrow is for her daughter, who is only a year old," Kathy said. "To be honest, I think the whole special preview day of the carnival is a bit over-the-top."

Laurel was one of Samantha's friends from high school, who also knew Kathy. After high school, Laurel met her husband, Charles, during her first year of college. He and his family lived in a large home on one of the tree-lined streets off of South Shore Drive, near Frontier Park. After Laurel had dropped out of college to get married, Samantha wondered whether Laurel had married for love or wealth.

Regardless, Laurel was now a mother to a beautiful one-year-old daughter named Ashley. And thanks to the deep pockets of her husband's family, Ashley was going to get a huge birthday bash that likely cost loads of money. Never mind the fact that Ashley probably wouldn't ever remember it.

"Well, that's Laurel's style now," Samantha said. "But it'll be fun. Even if we're the only two kid-less people there."

"Technically, *I'm* the only one without a kid," Kathy said. "Yours is just still cooking."

Samantha laughed and rubbed her belly. "Don't remind me."

"Can we talk about how weird a carnival party is for a one-year-old?" Kathy draped a pair of pants over her arm that she thought Samantha might like. "Is it for the kid or is it to show off in front of the neighbors?"

"The carnival was going to be in town anyway," Samantha explained. "Laurel just paid for a private preview a day early for her party."

"I'm sure that cost a pretty penny."

Shrugging, Samantha moved on to another rack. "I'm still debating whether I want to announce my pregnancy tomorrow. It all depends on what I'm wearing."

"I thought since you were past the first trimester and have a lower chance of miscarrying that you were more confident in the pregnancy?" Kathy came beside her sister and pushed away a pair of pants she was considering. "Not those—you're going to be a mother, not a grandmother."

Ignoring her sister's jab, Samantha walked over to the shoe

department and sat on a bench. Immediately, she felt relief in her feet, which had swollen after a day of shopping. "I am, but I'm still not sure. I don't want to steal Ashley's thunder."

"She's only a year old and her mother got her a carnival for her birthday. She's going to be overshadowed *just* a smidge."

Samantha shrugged her agreement.

"Besides, I'm just happy that it's been three months since we've had any sort of magical crisis."

"Knock on wood!" Samantha waved her finger at her sister. "Every time we assume that, something always comes up. I would like to make it through my pregnancy and the first six months of my child's life without having to chase down any bad guys."

"First of all, that year-and-a-half stretch is *seriously* wishful thinking. Something's bound to come up. Even so, I think we're safe for this weekend. I mean, what's going to happen at a baby's birthday party? Is a clown going to jump out and scare us? Doesn't exactly sound like something we'd need to take care of."

Samantha shook her head. "Stranger things have happened."

CHAPTER 4

The man quickly realized he needed to take a human form.

That was the first lesson.

The second lesson came when he crossed the Bayfront Parkway and nearly caused an accident. Apparently clothing was required for these humans as well. So when he continued down Greengarden Boulevard, he conjured up a set of clothes to cover himself.

But something still didn't quite feel right. It became apparent when he reached West 8th Street and caught several people at the gas station on the corner staring at him. He had messed up his appearance again somehow.

He stared at them and ran his hands over his body to figure out what he had missed. Right height, right number of appendages, right—oh, that was it. He forgot to add a nose.

It was just as well. Sometimes it was easier to take over someone else's identity and mimic their appearance. At that point, the hard work had all been done. They had a name, face, and people in their lives. Much easier to blend in that way.

The sun had begun to rise as the man made it to Cherokee Drive. He had no destination in mind. He was wandering the many residential streets near the large park. The more he walked, the more he saw cars driving in the street, joggers getting their morning exercise, and men in business suits taking their dogs for a stroll. The humans were waking up to start the day.

Any one of these people could be his new identity. But none of them seemed to interest him until—

Down the driveway of a brick colonial, the man saw another man in the garage. Beside the family car sat a bright pink tricycle.

A child's.

The man smiled and walked down the driveway to the other man. He wore a white dress shirt and a black tie, which he held against himself as he struggled to pull the trash bin out of the garage.

"Need any help with that?"

The man in the tie looked up. "I should be okay. Thanks."

"Nonsense, let me lend a hand. No trouble at all!" The

man held a smile on his face until he stepped into the garage with the man in the tie. Then, with a swiftness the man in the tie didn't see coming, he conjured and lunged a knife right into his stomach.

The man in the tie coughed, choking on his own blood as he sunk to his knees, then fell onto the concrete.

"I'm sorry," the man said. "I really hate to waste food, but I needed a cover. A place to lay low until I can regain my strength. You understand, right?"

When the man on the ground didn't answer, he laughed. "Look at me! I'm talking to a dead man!"

He gave the garage a closer inspection. There was only one car, but along the wall beside the tricycle there was a wooden box filled with outdoor children's toys. Through the window in the garage, the man could see a small shed in the back corner of the yard that had flowers painted on it.

Turning back to the dead man, he said, "Well, I see you have a family. So I better get this show on the road."

Grabbing the man's arms, he dragged him along the passenger side of the car and deeper into the garage. There, he looked around for a place to stash the body. Along the back wall there was a work bench with a sliding wooden door at the bottom. It was a tight fit, but the man figured it could work.

Hoisting the dead man up, he shoved him into the work bench, creating a mess with all of the blood. When he was finished, he managed to wedge the door shut. Unfortunately, there was still the matter of the blood. It was all over the concrete.

The man sighed. "Well, what are we going to do about this?"

"Morning!" A passerby on the sidewalk called.

Hidden deep in the garage, the man waved back politely until the neighbor walked on. Then, he muttered to himself, "First thing's first, I need to take care of the reason I chose you to begin with."

In an instant, his form had changed to look exactly like the man he had just killed—clothing and all. Nobody would be able to tell the difference.

Then, he stepped to one of the cabinets against the wall near the outdoor toys and dug around looking for cleaning supplies.

"Aren't you going to be late to work?" a woman asked suddenly behind him.

The man jumped and turned. "I—uh, I made a mess." He indicated the stains, preparing himself to conjure a knife again. Women tended to be screamers, so he didn't want to kill her. Besides, it really would've been a shame to waste even more food.

"From the trash?" she asked. "I got some chicken and steaks and stuff that I trimmed and put in the freezer. The packaging from all of that must've leaked through the bag. It's going to stink if we don't clean it up."

"Yeah, that's what I was trying to do."

She sighed. "I guess I'll have to pull out the hose and see if I can scrub some of it away. But you should get to work before Karen yells at you again. God knows we don't need you losing your job. Not if we want anymore kids."

The man smiled at the mention of kids, but he forced himself to play the part. He leaned in and kissed the woman, then stepped into the car. Once inside, he realized her forgot to take the keys away from the man before he stuffed his body in the work bench. No matter, he conjured a new set of keys, smiled at the wife, then started the engine and began to back out of the driveway.

"A child to feast on and a woman to clean up my mess," he said as he drove away. "I certainly lucked out with this one."

CHAPTER 5

Even though Kathy thoroughly enjoyed her day of shopping with her sister, ending up back at the mall for the evening shift at the store was not something she looked forward to. In fact, Ronnie had been scheduling her for evening shifts exclusively now. It was something that Kathy had requested when she was still taking classes, but now that the semester was over Kathy didn't need her mornings free anymore. For once, she wanted to be able to go home and enjoy the evening like Samantha and Steven did with their regular daytime jobs.

"Oooh, girl!" Leslie called to Kathy from behind the checkout counter. "You're looking like totally rad lately!"

Kathy couldn't help but smile as she pinned on her name tag and joined Leslie behind the counter. "I started running now that the weather's nicer."

In truth, Kathy had started running because of how often they needed to chase after bad guys. Now that Samantha was pregnant, she knew she would need to pick up the slack with their magical responsibilities. Being in shape would help with that.

"Oh, I know! Your mornings off have been doing *wonders* for you, girl." Leslie inspected Kathy up and down and then laughed. "Seriously, you look good."

"Yeah, but these evening shifts have been running me ragged."

"They cutting into your time with your boo?"

"No, we still make time for each other," Kathy said. "Actually, most days I meet him for lunch before I come here."

"That's nice. I noticed there haven't been any flower deliveries in a while."

"Yeah, the honeymoon phase with him has faded a bit, but that's okay. I don't need grand gestures to know my worth."

Ronnie walked over with a pile of clothes and plopped them on the counter. "Ladies, if you have time to lean, you have time to clean. Here, fold these and put them away, please. I just pulled all of this out of the fitting rooms. Leslie, you were supposed to do that earlier."

"And we got busy," Leslie said. "But don't you worry, Ronnie. I'll take care of it right now."

Their manager offered a tense smile and then walked off.

"I don't know what bug got in her pants, but she's been in a mood all day."

Kathy reached for the pile and began refolding. "Sales must be down. She always freaks when that happens."

"The Memorial Day sale this weekend will pick things up again," Leslie said. "Are you working it?"

"Sunday and Monday. Somehow, I got tomorrow and Saturday off."

"Lucky you. Ronnie hates me."

"She doesn't *hate* you, she just…" Kathy trailed off, lost for the ending of the sentence. Instead, she tried a diversion, "Anyway, as I was saying before we were interrupted, things with me and Jeremy are good."

"Not great?" Leslie folded a pair of men's swim trunks and piled them to the side.

"Things don't have to be great all the time."

Leslie looked at Kathy with an eyebrow raised. "Honey, this is *at least* your second time around with this guy. And you're only three months in! If the spark is gone already, then did it ever really exist?"

"We're just at different places in our lives," Kathy explained. "From when we first dated to now. And even now, he's working a full-time job and I'm still in school. It's just challenging, that's all."

"Challenging in what way?"

Kathy sighed and folded a pair of Guess jeans. "Sometimes,

I just feel like I'm still a kid while he's moved on to become an adult. And it's only worse with Samantha being married and having the baby." She shrugged. "I guess I just feel like I'm lagging behind. Like I need to step it up."

"Aw, honey. You'll get there. When you finish college and—"

Kathy groaned. "I don't even want to *think* about college."

"Why's that? You're doing good!"

"I still haven't picked a major. It's been a year and my advisor is pushing me to decide on something, but I still don't know what. And heaven forbid they help me figure it out!"

"Have you done any internships or job shadowing?"

"Not even sure what career field to start looking in. Everything I consider, I can't imagine doing for the rest of my life. Doing the same thing every day, forty hours a week…I don't know. It just seems so…restricting."

Leslie laughed. "Well, I don't disagree with that, but it is the way the world works. If you want to win at life, you kind of need to play the game."

"Yeah, yeah, yeah."

"In the meantime, though, you should talk to Jeremy—and Samantha. If you're feeling in their shadow, then maybe they can help you find your calling."

The trouble with that was, Kathy knew what her true calling was: being a witch. But that didn't pay the bills.

Once the clothes were folded, Kathy spent the first half of her shift putting them away. She also busied herself with straightening the displays and helping an old woman reach for the size she was looking for.

At that point, Leslie's shift had ended, leaving Kathy and the rest of the evening crew. As Kathy ventured back to the register, Ronnie called out to her from across the store, "Kathy! Go on break!"

Kathy had just stepped into the concourse after punching out and nearly collided with Trisha, who was running toward her with a skip in her step.

"Are you leaving?" Trisha grabbed Kathy's arms.

"Just getting something to eat," she said. "I'm on break."

"Good! I need to talk to you!"

CHAPTER 6

The man figured five o'clock was a reasonable time to return back to the house. He had spent the day driving around town, getting a feel for the area. It didn't seem like a bad city to settle in for a bit before he regained his strength.

He pulled into the garage and saw remnants of the stain on the concrete, but the woman had done a decent job cleaning it up. And all before the body in the work bench began to rot!

Before he left the garage, he inspected the work bench closer and saw that there was a small pile of juices collecting near the track of the sliding door. He'd have to move the body soon in order to maintain his cover.

He stepped inside and the woman breathed a sigh of relief.

"Oh good, you're home," she said. "Ashley! Daddy's home!"

She turned back to him, kissed him quickly on the lips. "Sorry to give you daughter duty right away, but I haven't had a chance to unpack from my trip to the store today. My head is spinning getting ready for this party tomorrow."

The man watched as she stepped into the kitchen, where plastic bags filled with party balloons, colorful tablecloths, and plastic silverware sat.

"The garage looks good," he offered. "Thanks for cleaning it."

"Yeah, I wanted to talk to you about that," she said. "The garage smells *terrible*. You need to remember to put the trash out early enough so it doesn't stink in there. I purposely try to put really stinky stuff in there the night before garbage day so it doesn't smell too bad."

The man thought about the body. Luckily, she hadn't discovered it. Now he would really have to move. "Sorry."

"It's okay. We'll just need to air it out." She quickly changed the subject. "Anyway, I picked up the cake. It looks delicious. I have it in the fridge down in the basement so nothing happens to it. Oh, and I heard from Bill and Sue, they're coming with the kids. And Marla called. Apparently Nathan is allergic to wheat, so I have to come up with alternatives for him."

The man had no idea who she was talking about, but he smiled and nodded.

"Oh, and the carnival manager called and confirmed that we're all set for tomorrow!" She clapped her hands. "It's going to be great! Ashley's going to love it! It's going to be a special preview day, just for us."

"You mean…the three of us?"

"No, everyone at the party! All the kids will love it!"

"Right, the kids." He had to force himself not to smile at the prospect of children. Kids had a habit of being scared by everything. And they always screamed the loudest. If he could maintain his patience, the reward could be amazing.

"I know you were complaining about the price, but I really do think it'll be a great first birthday party for her." She came over and kissed him again. "You're such a good dad."

From the next room over, a baby began to wail.

"Speak of the devil," the woman said with a smile. "She must've woken up from her little nap. Do you mind getting her and putting her in the high chair before you go up to change? I want to give her a little snack before dinner because I have no idea when I'm going to get to making that with everything else I need to do."

"No problem." He followed the sound of the crying, which stopped when he entered the living room.

The curtains were pulled closed and there were toys all over the floor. In the corner sat a playpen where a little girl with blonde hair stood with her hands on the edge.

"Well, hello there you little scrumptious girl." As the man got closer to her, the little girl began to wail, screaming at the top of her lungs. The man reached for her, picking her up despite her cries. She swatted at him, continuing to screech her protests.

"What is it? What's going on?" The woman rushed into the room.

"I don't know," he answered honestly. "She just started screaming."

"Come here, sweetie," the woman said in a baby voice.

As the girl was taken by her mother, she clung to her tightly, giving nervous glances to the man before turning back to her mother.

"How weird," the woman muttered to the man. "She must be cranky today."

The man clenched his jaw. The damn kid probably sensed that he wasn't truly her father. Adults were often more oblivious than children.

"Come on, let's get you something to eat." The woman carried the girl back to the kitchen.

When they were out of earshot, the man muttered, "Don't you blow my cover, little girl."

CHAPTER 7

Samantha sat on the floor of the spare bedroom and sifted through an old box that had been stashed in the closet ever since their father had left. Steven, meanwhile, worked in the closet, pulling out boxes and bags and anything else the girls had stuck in there and forgotten about.

"This place is a mess!"

"It's kind of been our catch-all room since we've taken ownership of the house," Samantha said. "Other than the closet, I feel like we maintained a fairly decent guest bedroom."

Steven raised his eyebrows. "Who knew you had this much crap stashed in here?"

"Crap or treasures?" Samantha held up what had once been her pet rock and smiled.

TRICKSTER

Weeks ago, they had set this date after work to clean out the spare bedroom so they could get it ready to turn into a nursery. It was a task neither of them looked forward to, but it needed to get done.

"Who's room did this used to be?" Steven pulled down several old shoeboxes from the top shelf of the closet. He stacked them in the corner with the shoeboxes that had been stashed under the bed.

"Kathy's," Samantha said. "We played musical rooms when it became obvious Dad wasn't coming back. I took his room, Kathy took my old room. Since this is the smallest bedroom, it became the guest room." Then, in an effort to glaze over her father's absence in the wake of their growing family, Samantha asked, "What's a good gender-neutral color for this room?"

Steven looked around. "You don't want to find out the sex of the baby beforehand? We could paint it blue or pink."

"I don't want to go overboard with those colors. If the walls are neutral, we can furnish the room with blue or pink…or whatever other colors we choose. It's not like the baby's going to care."

"Well, they will eventually."

"And by that point, they can decide."

Steven smiled. Samantha loved how excited her husband was about the arrival of their baby. Even though the pregnancy had come along much sooner than either of them had expected—and even though Samantha was still nervous about how she was going to continue her witch career with a newborn—she couldn't help but be excited too.

"That's everything." Steven put his hands on his hips and looked up and down the empty closet. "It needs to be vacuumed and dusted, but I can get that done once we figure out where all this junk is going. What's even in all these shoeboxes anyway?" He lifted the lid of one and found a bunch of old cassette tapes.

"Different things," Samantha said. "My dad used to say my mom insisted on keeping all of her old shoeboxes because it was the perfect organizational storage." She shrugged. "It worked for a while, but I'm ready to get rid of them if there's nothing special in them. If we haven't used it in the last five or six years, we're not going to need it again."

"Do you want to go through all these?"

"I'm working on this larger box." The box beside her was stashed at the bottom of the closet and contained photo albums and picture frames. She hadn't done a deep-dive into it yet, too distracted by her conversation with Steven. "You can go through the shoeboxes, see if there's anything Kathy or I might want."

"Yes ma'am."

Samantha reached in her box and pulled out several gaudy frames. Most of them were cracked or broken. One, in particular, had shattered, leaving shards of glass in the bottom of the box. Carefully, Samantha moved the frames aside and pulled out the large photo album tomes at the bottom.

Brushing off the dust, she set it in her lap and began to flip through. She saw old faded pictures of her and Kathy as infants, then as toddling babies. Samantha's heart fluttered when she saw a picture of her mother, holding baby Samantha's hands while she struggled to walk for the first time.

"Have you thought of any names?" Steven asked.

"Huh?" Samantha blinked away the tears and looked up at her husband. "Um…names? Sort of. Have you?"

He shrugged. "I've been thinking a little. What are yours?"

"You first."

"Well, if it's a girl, I was thinking Leah. And if it's a boy, Patrick."

Samantha rocked her head back and forth. "Those aren't terrible, I suppose."

"What have you come up with?"

"For a girl, I was thinking Tracy. And for a boy, Joshua—or Josh."

"Josh?"

"What's wrong with Josh? You don't like that name?"

"I mean, I guess it's fine. It's not my top pick, but it's not one I'd veto."

"Let it marinate in that mind of yours," Samantha said with a smirk. "I'm sure it'll grow on you."

Steven opened another shoebox. "You girls are going to have to go through this one. It's jam-packed with jewelry."

"Probably all junk, honestly," Samantha said. "Kathy was very into over-accessorizing in middle school. But we can take a look at it. Set it aside for now."

Samantha also set aside the photo albums. She had caught a glimpse of her mother, which she loved, but it also brought about immense sadness. Unlike her father, who chose not to return to them, Samantha's mother had died young and missed out on her and Kathy's childhoods. And now, as adults, their mother was missing out on other milestones in their lives as well. It wasn't fair. The more pregnant Samantha became, the more she began to understand the enormity of growing up without a mother. It brought up feelings she didn't even know she had.

"You know, there was something else I've been thinking about," Steven said as he closed up another shoebox and set it in a pile.

"What's that?"

"This baby is half you and half me."

"That's kind of how genetics work, yes."

"So does that mean the baby will be…you know…um, a witch, like you?"

The hesitation was evident in his voice. Samantha being a witch was one of Steven's least favorite qualities of her, she knew. He put up with it, but that's because Samantha had the experience to take care of herself in dangerous situations. The baby was another story.

With the memory of her own fractured family fresh on her mind, Samantha decided that it would be best to keep the peace and cross the magical bridge when the time came.

"Uh…not necessarily," she said. "He or she could be nonmagical, just like you."

"Oh okay. So it's like hair color or eye color? They get one or the other, not a mix of both? We'll just have to wait and see."

"I guess so," she said. "This is my first baby. I'm not exactly sure how it works."

That, of course, was a lie. She knew that the chances of their baby not having any trace of magic was slim. More than likely, their baby would have the same magical abilities as its mother. Samantha was just worried that if their baby had magic, Steven would finally have enough of the magical life and leave. And she didn't want her child to grow up with only one parent like she had.

CHAPTER 8

The food court was fairly loud considering that it was a Thursday night. But then, Kathy remembered, it was just before the long Memorial Day weekend. Kids didn't have school the next four days, so many of them must've opted for a jump start to their weekend by hanging out at the mall.

Carrying her salad bowl over to a clean table, Kathy waited for Trisha to return with her tray from Burger King.

"No Whopper?" Trisha asked as she took a seat.

Kathy shook her head. "Trying to eat healthier." She opened the top of her salad and began to dive in.

"Didn't realize you were on a diet. But then, you've lost a lot of weight. Are you sure you're eating enough?"

"Actually, I feel much better than I have in a long time,"

Kathy said. "And it's not a diet. I'm just trying not to eat such fatty, sugary things."

Trisha picked up her burger and shrugged. "Suit yourself."

"I really only lost, like, ten pounds."

"Well, you look tiny."

Kathy was already tired of the comments about her body. "What is it you wanted to talk to me about?"

"Mmm!" Trisha's eyes got wide and she held up a finger as she finished chewing. "I got a new job!"

"You did? Where?"

"The Hamot Medical Center! More pay, more responsibility, better job security, the whole thing."

"Benefits?"

Trisha scrunched her eyebrows. "I didn't even ask about that. I assume so. I'll have to check into that. Anyway, I thought of you!"

"Why?"

"Because now there's an opening at my current job!"

Kathy stabbed her lettuce and dipped it in the dressing that had collected at the bottom of the plastic bowl. "What is it you do again?"

"I'm a receptionist at Dr. Newberg's office. It's right by the high school, between Cherry and Peach Streets. So it's close enough that you could walk to if you needed to."

"I don't think I'm qualified for—"

"They're having a hard time finding someone to replace me,

so they're going to post the position again. Honestly, Dr. Newberg and his staff have been so good to me and I wish I wasn't leaving, but I need to step up in the world, you know?"

She paused to dig something out of her bag, which she had set on the floor beside her seat. A moment later, she slapped a job application in front of her.

"Anyway, I thought you would be perfect for it," she went on. "I would feel so much better for them if I could help them find a competent person to take my place, plus it'd be a great opportunity for one of my good friends!"

Kathy eyed the application. "I don't need any kind of credentials?"

"They'll train you! And quickly, because the patient caseload is building. That's what made the decision to leave so difficult, but I think this will be a good move for me. I really do. And you're almost done with an associate's, right? How are your classes going?"

Kathy made a face. "They're okay. I still haven't picked a major, so I'm not actually on track for any degree. I'm just kind of taking classes."

"Oh. Well, those credits should count for something. Maybe this job will help you figure out what major to declare."

"Maybe." It would at least give her an area to try out to see if she'd like working in the medical field. She never thought she'd be doing that, but life had a way of putting her in situations she never thought she'd be in.

"You could even finish up part time," Trisha said. "Dr. Newberg will let you work full time and will support whatever class schedule you have. He did it when I was in school."

"What are the hours?"

"Monday through Friday, nine to five."

Kathy raised her eyebrows and nodded. "That does sound tempting. And it's salaried?"

"Technically hourly, but you'll be guaranteed forty hours. Well, forty minus breaks. What is that? Like, thirty-seven?"

"And the pay is more than minimum?"

Trisha nodded. "A little above. You start at four dollars an hour."

"Oh wow. That's pretty good."

"Yeah, and there's annual raises, based on performance."

Kathy finished up the rest of her salad. She grabbed the application and sat back in her seat as she looked it over. "It's tempting, that's for sure."

"What's holding you back?"

"I don't know. It's just that I wasn't expecting this change."

"Doesn't mean it's a bad thing." Trisha wiped the ketchup from her lips with a napkin. "Sometimes the best things in life are surprises."

"True. I mean, I think a change is necessary. To be honest, I've been feeling a little juvenile compared to Jeremy lately. He's got this nice real job and I'm still working at the mall and taking classes."

Trisha crumpled up her wrappers and waved off Kathy's comment. "Don't worry about him. You need to live your life regardless of what everyone else is doing. You'll get where you need to be eventually."

Kathy nodded. She'd heard that before and, deep down, she believed it. Over these last ten months, she'd been trying to be the person everyone else wanted her to be. She'd taken college classes, maintained a job, helped with the bills.

But she'd struggled through it all. The classes were hard and not as rewarding as she thought they'd be. Her job was getting tedious and tiring. And she barely had enough to help pay the bills, especially if Samantha and Steven did eventually move out.

"I'm not pressuring you one way or another," Trisha said. "Just think about it."

CHAPTER 9

The man was elbow-deep in sudsy water as he cleaned the dishes in the sink. Beside him, the woman stood drying the dishes.

"So how many people are we expecting tomorrow?" he asked her.

"Oh gosh," she said. "Um…let's see…I'm thinking closer to fifty. Maybe a little more. Maybe a little less."

"And how many of those are kids?"

"Nervous you're going to have your hands full?" she asked with a grin. "Maybe fifteen kids. All different ages, though. From Ashley's age or younger up to—well, I think Marla's daughter is almost ten. I think she'd be the oldest out of tomorrow's group. Yeah, that sounds right."

The way she talked, the man wondered if the woman could carry on the conversation even if he was absent from the room. He suspected she might be able to. That just made blending in that much easier for him.

"I invited the whole neighborhood, as well as some of our other friends," she went on. "I figured, we're spending this money for the preview day at the carnival. We might as well get as many people as possible to enjoy it."

"It sounds like it'll be a great day," he said cheerfully. "All those kids will have loads of fun. Maybe we should even call up the kids from Ashley's daycare and invite them."

The woman was quiet for a moment until he looked at her. "What?"

"Ashley doesn't go to daycare," she said with a forced laugh. "Are you all right? You didn't seem that happy about this party before. Why the sudden change?"

He shrugged, kicking himself for overplaying the role. He needed to keep his head on straight if he was going to get what he wanted. "I'm just thinking, Ashley would love it. I mean, she's the only one around here and she needs other kids to play with."

"That's true." The woman opened a drawer and began setting the silverware in the correct places.

"I love seeing her happy." He reached for the faucet and turned off the water.

"You're a great dad," she said.

"Thanks. Hey, why don't I be a great husband and finish cleaning up here?"

She raised her eyebrows at him. "You're offering to clean the kitchen?"

"Well, the dishes at least."

She laughed. "That sounds more like you. And I'm not going to turn down that offer." She leaned up and kissed his cheek. "I'm going to bed. You want me to wait up?"

"Nah, I've got some other things to take care of after I finish in here."

Now in the doorway, she gave him a smile. "Okay. Just don't stay up too late. We have a busy day tomorrow."

"Wouldn't dream of it." He watched her disappear upstairs and busied himself with putting away the rest of the dishes, buying time for the woman to get situated upstairs. From his limited experience with humans, women tended to take longer getting ready. For anything.

When he was sure she was finally settled upstairs, he quietly went to the back door and stepped outside. The night was chilly, even though the day had been warm. With the snap of his fingers, he could change that in an instant. But he needed to conserve his energy.

Stepping into the dark garage, he opened up the wooden door on the work bench and was hit with the foul stench of the dead husband. The blood and other juices from his body had already seeped through the wood and were now dripping on the concrete floor. The warm day hadn't done any favors to the body.

"Time to put you in a much better resting place," the man murmured to the corpse.

Grabbing ahold of the body, he pulled until the cadaver fell with a *splat* on the concrete. Then, he grabbed the dead man's wrists and dragged him out through the yard toward the garden shed.

Halfway there, he saw something pass by the window upstairs where a light was still on. The woman appeared through the glass, oblivious to what was going on outside.

The man's heart raced as he watched, wondering if he was about to be discovered. Instead, she moved out of view and the room become a little dimmer as she turned off one of the bedside lamps.

Breathing a sigh of relief, he dragged the woman's husband the rest of the way across the yard.

The garden shed would only hold the stench a little longer than the garage did, but he only needed a little longer. By tomorrow, he'd be feasting on all those children and be back up to full strength.

CHAPTER 10

Too poofy. Too tight. Too bright.

Everything Samantha tried on, she seemed to hate. Her belly wasn't protruding too much yet, but she could tell that she was all-around thicker. It was her body's way of preparing to carry the baby for the duration of the pregnancy. Ordinarily, Samantha wasn't that concerned with her waistline, but for some reason this change in her body was bothering her at the moment.

"That's cute." Kathy walked into Samantha's room in a floral white sundress and lay on her stomach on Samantha's bed.

In the mirror, Samantha made a face. "I'm not sure." She had on a blue top that hung loosely in front of her. It was a different style than she was used to wearing, which was part of the reason she was so insecure about it.

"You look great, Sam. And with that top, nobody can tell that you're pregnant unless you decide to tell them."

Samantha turned and measured how much her tiny little baby bump was sticking out. Kathy was right. With the flowing blouse she was wearing, it was hard to see the true shape of her body.

"It's a good thing you got today off." Kathy inspected her freshly-painted nails on the bed.

Samantha held up other outfits and inspected them in the mirror, trying to determine whether the outfit she had on was the one she wanted to wear to Laurel's party. "I took the day off."

"Yeah. You deserve a break. It's why I'm so relieved that my classes are over for the semester."

"Mm-hmm." Samantha was only partially listening. She had determined that the one she was wearing was decent enough to wear. Now she needed to figure out how much makeup to wear.

"I don't know how you made it through four years of college full-time while also working several jobs," Kathy said behind her.

"Sometimes I wonder the same thing." Samantha grabbed her makeup bag from the top of her dresser and took a seat on the floor in front of her mirror. Her face seemed washed out. She'd been sleeping fairly well, but nausea and the extra body growing inside of her seemed to drain her energy. She'd need to cover that up.

"But if you had needed to take a break because we didn't have the money, what exactly was your plan?"

Samantha brushed on the mascara. "I would've just taken a semester off. Or shifted to part-time for a semester. Taken fewer credits or something like that. Luckily, I didn't need to do that. We cut it close a few times, but we managed." She screwed the brush back into the base and tossed it back into her bag. "Glad that part of my life is over. And now we're in a better place than we were when I went to school, so you have nothing to worry about."

"Yeah," Kathy murmured. She was quiet a moment, then said, "I guess I'm just a little bored."

"With what?"

"My job. It's all right, but it's not what I want to do forever."

"Sure, but it's what you need to do right now."

"I'm thinking finding a new one might help me feel better."

Samantha shot her sister a look in the mirror, then turned back to her makeup bag. "Of course. It's been almost a year. About time you found something new."

"What's that supposed to mean?"

"A year is usually about how long you last at any job. You work somewhere for about a year—*if* you make it that long— and then you move on to something else. It's like you have an expiration date or something."

Kathy sat up. "Hey, I've had a lot on my plate this last year. Not everyone needs to be a workaholic like you. Some of us actually want to *enjoy* life instead of just *get through* it."

Samantha sighed, realizing how insensitive she had been. "I'm sorry. You're right. You've taken on a lot and I'm proud of you for that. It's just that, up until now, you haven't had the best track record. I'm just thinking of your résumé when you finish school and start applying to real, full-time jobs. They're going to look at how long you can keep a job when they decide to hire you. Plus, you're going to have to hold down a job for a long time when it's the only thing paying the bills. You can't just keep jumping around."

"I know that I have to keep a job," she said. "And it's not like I'd quit before I had something else lined up. I actually—"

"Kathy, I don't want to argue before the party." Samantha tossed the last of her makeup in her bag and zipped it closed. She rose to her feet and gave one final look in the mirror. She sighed. "I guess I'm as ready to go as I'll ever be. How about you?"

Sighing, Kathy pushed off the bed and got to her feet. "Yeah. I'll meet you downstairs."

CHAPTER 11

The sisters walked up to the picnic area set up at Frontier Park with Steven in tow. Typically, the park was just a large open green space with tennis courts, a playground, and a soccer field in one end of the park. Today, however, there were several large yellow and pink tents set up in a group just off West 8th Street. Beyond that grouping of tents was a makeshift picnic area with foldable card tables, lawn chairs, and portable grills, where there were already a fair number of people talking and laughing with small children running around.

"Samantha!" Laurel gave an exaggerated smile. She raised her hands in the air as she raced toward her, wrapping her arms around her. She wore a white button-up blouse tucked into her high-waisted jeans. "It's so good to *see* you! Oh, and Kathy!" Laurel turned her attention to the younger sister and hugged her as well. "Gosh, you look amazing!"

Kathy smiled. "Thank you. So do you."

Laurel feigned modesty. "Well, I've been reading Elizabeth Taylor's book and following her dieting advice. Veggies and dip at three o'clock sharp, every afternoon!"

Kathy nodded politely. "Very nice."

"This is my husband, Steven." Samantha put her hand on his arm as she introduced him.

Laurel shook his hand, then turned back to Samantha. "I didn't realize you got married! How wonderful!"

"Yup, about four months ago now," Samantha said with a smile.

Behind them, a gust of wind came through and flipped one of the card tables right over, sending drinks and bowls of chips all over the lawn. Several adults jumped to clean it up.

"You got that okay, honey?" Laurel called back to her husband, Charles. He gave a wave and she turned back to Samantha. "He's got it. Strangely enough, that's been happening all day."

"Well, I mean, we're in an open field, basically," Samantha said. "The wind carries, especially this close to the lake." It was only a few blocks away.

Laurel pursed her lips. "Very true. Anyway, any kids in your future?"

Samantha figured it was better to tell her than to not. "Well, actually—"

"Oh my gosh, stop!" Laurel placed both hands on the sides of her face as her mouth drew out into a large "O." Then she reached out and touched Samantha's stomach without warning.

"Oh. Okay then," Samantha murmured.

"You have a little bump! Oh my goodness, how cute is that!" Laurel was talking rather loudly and Samantha wondered if she would go on blabbing the news to everyone at the party. Other than Laurel, Samantha didn't see anyone else that she knew.

"Yeah, this came along a lot sooner than we expected." Steven rubbed his wife's back and beamed with pride. "But we're super excited."

"I bet!" Laurel made a pouty face, which almost immediately turned into a smile so bright that there was no way it could be genuine. "Oh, Sammy! I'm so happy for you!" She turned to Kathy. "What about you? Married?"

She shook her head, again offering a polite smile. "No, not yet."

"Oh, well, you'll get there." Without another moment wasted, Laurel turned back to Samantha and flashed her mega-watt smile. "Gosh, what a ride you two are in for! My Ashley is a year now and on one hand it seems like she was just born and yet on the other hand, it's like, it's only been a year?" She laughed loudly. "Oh, but motherhood is *great*. Truly a gift."

"Well, I'm looking forward to it," Samantha said. "A little nervous, but mostly excited."

"You should be! It is, like, the most rewarding thing I've

done in my *entire* life. Really amazing." She waved the air in front of her. "Anyway! I shouldn't keep you from the party. Come on and say hi to everyone! Oh, but make sure you call me if you have *any* questions once the baby comes. Or before! I can answer pregnancy questions too!"

Samantha nodded. "I'll do that."

Laurel hooked one arm around Samantha's shoulders then waved in the air toward her husband. "Charles! *Charles!* Come and meet Samantha!"

"Do you know what happened to my tongs?" he asked.

"They should be with the grill," Laurel said.

"I checked. They're not there. Did you leave them in the car?"

"The car's empty. You must've misplaced them somewhere."

"I'm not the one who pulled out the grill!" Charles said. "Maybe you dropped them in the lawn when you pulled it out."

"I didn't *drop* anything, Charles." Laurel forced a smile. "Maybe you're not *looking* hard enough."

He threw up his arms. "Whatever. How am I supposed to cook the burgers and hot dogs if I don't have any tongs?"

"Then *I guess*," she said through gritted teeth and a forced smile, "that you're going to have to run home."

Meanwhile, Samantha remained locked beside her friend, uncomfortably close to their marital argument.

Steven and Kathy followed behind, although they stayed far enough back for Steven to murmur to Kathy, "How did Jeremy get out of coming?"

"He had to work," Kathy said. "New job. Doesn't have time off yet."

"I should've used that excuse."

"I don't think that would work on my sister," Kathy said.

In front of them, Laurel became momentarily distracted when one little girl approached her to ask where the drinks were. Samantha took that opportunity to turn back to her husband.

"Besides, I would've used my pregnancy to guilt you into coming."

Kathy looked up at Steven and grinned. "Looks like you were stuck either way."

CHAPTER 12

For the most part, Samantha, Kathy, and Steven kept to themselves during the party. None of them knew very many of the other people in attendance, making it difficult to mingle and chitchat. To make matters worse, they were the only adults at the party who didn't have small children to tend to.

Most of the kids were running back and forth between the picnic area and the carnival. They were laughing and yelling and chasing each other. Some of them had overprotective parents chasing behind, calling for them to "Slow down," "Be nice," or "Drink some water."

They set up their lawn chairs to the side, but still within the groupings of the others. When they first chose the spot, Samantha's chair ripped in half when she tried to sit in it, which did nothing to help her mood or her image of her own body. Steven offered up his chair and he sat in the grass. The chivalry did little to help Samantha feel any better and the three of them sat in tense silence, each of them wondering how soon would be too soon to go home and forget they ever came to this party.

"All right, I'm going to get something to drink." Kathy rose to her feet and looked between Samantha and Steven. "Do you guys want anything?"

"No thanks," Samantha murmured.

From the ground, Steven shook his head. "I'm all set, thanks."

"Suit yourself." With a shrug, Kathy turned and wandered off toward the coolers under the folding card tables Laurel had brought.

"How am I already a whale?" Samantha asked.

"What?" Steven asked.

"I mean, I'm only a few months pregnant and I'm huge. I'm a whale."

"You're not a whale, honey."

"Aren't I? Laurel knew I was pregnant from a mile away. And don't forget the chair crumpling under my massive weight. What a way to announce to everyone how fat I am."

Steven had to stifle a smile at the memory of Samantha crashing to the ground through the aluminum chair. "Sam, I think you look great."

"Of course you do. You did this to me."

From the coolers, they could hear Laurel saying to a stranger, "Look at Kathy! Doesn't she look amazing?"

He sighed. "You're carrying a baby. Naturally, your body is going to change."

"So that means I'm supposed to lose all of my appearances just so I can create life? I mean, what the hell? Why bother trying at all? Let me just sit with my feet up and eat whatever the hell I want. It's not like I can control what my body's doing anyway."

At the group of chairs beside them, someone opened a can of pop and it exploded all over their face.

"I just feel like I'm sacrificing so much for this baby—who I want and I already love and I'm very happy for. I just wish I could be a mother without having to turn into a monster in the process."

"You're not a monster," Steven said. "It's just that you're a woman. That's how these things happen."

She glared at him. "If I'm giving up so much for our child, tell me, what is it that *you're* giving up?"

Steven stammered, searching for a response. Not just any response. The *correct* response. He was grateful to be saved by Kathy's return.

"Jeez, doesn't it seem like this whole place is cursed?" the younger sister asked as she retook her seat—slowly leaning into it so as to test its ability to hold her weight.

Samantha rolled her eyes. "Okay, Miss Model, it's not like

you have anything to worry—"

Piercing screams erupted from one of the tents at the carnival, and everyone's eyes turned in that direction.

CHAPTER 13

The man played the perfect husband role at the party. He sipped from his can of pop, laughed when jokes were told, greeted guests, encouraged people to eat, and even prepared the food for them.

Meanwhile, he watched the kids as they ran around. As they laughed. As they whined. As they begged their parents for one thing or another.

Annoying, they all were, but oh how tasty! As he surveyed them all, he tried to pick out which one he would target first. He had already checked out the funhouse tent. It would be the perfect place to feast. Anyone who entered expected gimmicks. His power would fit there perfectly without anyone being the wiser.

Unfortunately, he had already run into one hiccup. He thought that he could distract his fake wife by making the grilling tongs disappear. Maybe get her to run home and grab some more. The house wasn't far from the park. It wouldn't take her long. But it would be long enough for him to sneak away for some…appetizers.

Except, she didn't take the bait. She was stubborn when it came to appearances with other people and he resented her for that. In fact, he would need to think up an exceptionally cruel torture for her once he was able to get back up to full strength.

As the party went on, the man grew frustrated. The woman he came with insisted that everyone eat before they were allowed to go to the carnival. And she wanted to wait for everyone to arrive and get settled before they rushed to make the food.

In the meantime, these kids were running around the man, so close and yet so far from him feasting on their fears. It was a form of torture in its own right.

To entertain himself as he waited, he looked for opportunities to cause chaos. As one woman went to sit in a chair, he rubbed the side of his nose and suddenly the lawn chair ripped beneath her, sending her crashing to the ground. The disdain on her face was worth the effort.

Shortly after that, a man in a Hawaiian shirt and khaki cargo shorts grabbed a can of pop from one of the coolers. The man scratched the back of his neck and when Hawaiian shirt popped open the can when he settled back into his chair, the can exploded in his face, sending sticky liquid all over everyone.

The man did his best not to snicker and give himself away.

Best of all his pranks, though, was the wind. It drove his fake wife mad each and every time. It took all of the man's effort not to burst out laughing. Every time she had the table set up with the plastic tablecloth, paper plates, plastic silverware, and cups, a mysterious gust of wind would come out of *nowhere* and blow everything around. The wind caused a frenzy with people chasing after pieces and trying to regain control of the items that they had brought to the park.

The man was about to cause one of the birthday balloons to explode in someone's face when he caught something out of the corner of his eye. One little girl was making a dash to the funhouse tent.

All by herself.

A smile curled on the man's lips. Showtime.

Closing his eyes for a moment, he duplicated himself, his copy materializing right in the center of the funhouse tent.

The copy—inside the tent—took the form of a clown, then knelt down in the center of the large room and waited.

The anticipation was almost too much to bear.

CHAPTER 14

Kelly was bored. So far the party was a bunch of grown-ups talking. There were some kids running around, but she didn't know them. And she couldn't be expected to play with kids she didn't know.

Besides, the carnival tents were calling to her to explore. They were bigger than any tent she had seen before and they were a beautiful bright yellow. The one closest to them said, "Funhouse," so she knew that would probably be the best one to try first.

She couldn't wait any longer. She needed to go see it for herself.

Tugging on her father's shirt, she asked, "Daddy, can I go to the funhouse?"

Her father knelt down beside her and looked to where she pointed. He turned back to the party and said, "It doesn't look like anyone else is going over there yet. Why don't you wait a few more minutes until everyone shows up?"

"But I want to go *now*!" she whined.

"I know, sweetie, but it's only fair to wait until everyone gets a turn."

She crossed her arms and huffed.

Her dad kissed the top of her head. "It shouldn't be too much longer, peanut." He rose back to his feet to continue his conversation with the other adults.

Kelly wandered toward a nearby tree to pout. He dad watched her walk away and waved to her when she sat against the trunk of the tree.

It wasn't fair. She wanted to see the funhouse. And she didn't want to have to wait. She didn't care about the other kids.

Glancing back at the party again, she saw her dad busy in his conversation. She looked over at the entrance to the tent. It wasn't too far away. If she ran fast—which she knew she could— she could sneak in without him knowing.

Keeping an eye on her dad, Kelly got to her feet. She inched toward the tent, testing the waters to see if someone would say something. Nobody did, so she broke into a run, not stopping or looking back until she was inside.

The tent was darker than she thought it would be, but she wasn't a wimp. And she wasn't scared.

Trickster

From the entrance, there were three different doorways to choose from. Kelly picked the one in the middle. When she came back later with her dad, they could try the other ones. He wouldn't be mad at her if she went through it with him later. Until then, she was anxious to find out what fun was held inside.

The pathway was darker than she expected. When she turned the first corner, there were funhouse mirrors lined against the tent walls down the hall all the way to the next turn.

Kelly stopped at each one, laughing and making faces at the funny expressions reflected back at her. This really was a fun house!

After having her fun with the mirrors, she moved on. The next few turns weren't as exciting. Boring, even. Kelly was disappointed that the tent was dark and empty. If she wanted to walk through a maze, she could've just waited until Halloween and asked her dad to take her to a corn maze.

Down the next hallway, things changed. To Kelly's surprise, she saw her mother standing there.

"Mommy!" She ran to the woman she hadn't seen in a long time, but her mother took a step back. When Kelly looked up, she saw a disgusted look on her mother's face.

"Don't touch me with those grubby little hands of yours!" she snapped. "You've probably been playing in the dirt again. You were, weren't you? You filthy little girl."

Kelly wrapped her arms around herself, feeling her lower lip push out. This wasn't surprising. Her mother had always been mean to her. But she thought it'd be different the next time they saw each other. Kelly thought she'd been good!

"Just leave me alone," her mother said. "I never wanted you to begin with."

With tears welling up in her eyes, Kelly turned and tried to run back to the entrance. To her father.

But the maze was different now. The path she had taken was not the same. The twists and turns were confusing and soon, Kelly found herself coming up to a corner that made her pause. She heard…hissing.

Peering around the corner, she saw a large pile of snakes all coiled together and blocking the path forward. One lunged at her feet and she nearly stumbled backward in her attempt to flee.

Screaming in fear, she turned and raced back. Even if her mother was mean, she would be able to help her find her way out. Maybe. Hopefully.

Except, her mother was no longer there. That didn't slow Kelly down, though, and she pressed on. She just wanted to get back outside and be with her dad. This house wasn't fun anymore.

Finally, she came to a large room. In the center, a clown sat on his feet, crying into his hands.

Kelly hated clowns. She didn't like the makeup or the big shoes or the puffy pants.

But he was crying. And Kelly knew what it was like to cry

and not have anyone comfort her. Slowly, she stepped forward.

"Hello," she said quietly.

The clown glanced at her, but continued to cry.

"What's wrong?" She took another step forward.

He turned away from her, keeping his face hidden.

"If something's bothering you, it's best to say it out loud," she said. "That's what my daddy says. When you say it out loud, someone can help you fix the problem."

The clown only continued to cry.

Kelly took another step. She was close enough that she could reach out and—

Her hand was quickly seized by the clown. She cried out, terrified now that she saw his painted face. Now that he leaned in closer to her, laughing—not crying—the harder she screamed.

CHAPTER 15

The crowd rushed to the sound of the scream, which came from within the funhouse tent. There was a large "Closed" sign over the main entrance, which apparently had gone unnoticed or ignored.

"My baby!" Laurel cried out in hysterics. "Who has my baby! Ashley! Come to Mommy!"

Samantha, Kathy, and Steven kept their distance at first, until it seemed that there was something keeping everyone from going inside the tent to trace down the scream, which still prevailed.

Kathy had to admit that the tent gave off a creepy vibe that gave her the chills, even in the warm sunlight.

"Ashley!" Laurel shouted when another mother carried over

the little one-year-old whose party this was for.

"We have to go in and see what's going on," Steven said.

The sisters nodded and the three of them were the first to lead other people inside.

Once they got through the front flap of the tent, they were faced with three different options.

"It's a maze," Samantha said.

"Like a haunted house," Kathy added.

"We'll have to split up," a man said from beside them. "Stay in groups. We don't know who's in there."

Everyone seemed to pair off. The sisters naturally clung to each other, leaving Steven and another man to venture through an opening together.

The sisters chose the third path, directly in the middle. The first long stretch seemed perfectly normal, even if the light seemed to get dimmer and dimmer the father away from the entrance they got. When they rounded the corner, however, the funhouse began.

Along the canvas walls of the tent there were clown faces painted, which were supposed to be different levels of cheer. In the gloom, however, the faces seemed more sinister than joyful.

"I didn't realize people still liked clowns," Kathy murmured. "They seem kind of...creepy."

"Trust me, my baby will never have any clowns in their room," Samantha said.

Around another corner, the sisters entered into a larger

space. At first, they saw the standard funhouse mirrors, warped to show distorted reflections.

Samantha walked up to one, which exaggerated her hips. She groaned. "I don't think I thought through this whole motherhood thing. If this is what I'm going to look like in twenty years, I don't want it."

Kathy rolled her eyes. "That's not what you *actually* look like, Sam."

"Still—"

Above them, bright lights began to flash on and off, reflecting off the mirrors and blinding the girls. From above them, they heard the maniacal laugh of a clown on a loop.

With eyes closed tight, the sisters reached out and felt for each other until they had firm grasps on one another's hands.

"Do you know where the exit is?" Kathy called over the looping laughter.

"No! Let's find a wall and figure it out from there."

With her free hand extended, Samantha led her sister several small steps toward the edge. They moved slowly, so as not to crash into anything. Finally, her hand brushed against the cold, smooth surface of the funhouse mirror glass, just as the strobe lights shut off above them.

"Holy hell, how does anyone find that enjoyable?" Kathy asked.

"Isn't that kind of the same thing as what you do at the club?"

"That's different," she said. "Besides, I haven't been to one in almost a year. Not sure I want to now."

Samantha pointed to an opening that was different from the one they came through. "This way."

The rest of the labyrinth was less eventful. The canvas was painted in optical illusions, making it difficult to navigate the pathway, but otherwise it wasn't too exciting. The sisters navigated the winding hallways, choosing different crossroads based on the sound of the cries coming from the little girl.

At last, they came upon a larger room, where they saw the little girl laying in the grass with a clown hovering over her. As the girl screamed, light shone from the girl's face to the clown's.

"Hey!" Samantha called out. The sound of the voice made the light transferring from the girl to the clown cease immediately.

Turning, the clown faced them, making both girls gasp. Instead of a cheerful smile, like the ones that had been alluded to along the walls of the tent, this clown had a sinister stare. His white painted face only accentuated his large yellow teeth that seemed to be sharpened to points, made to rip and tear flesh. Even his poofy pants and large shoes were a dingy yellow, reminiscent of clothes that had been stored in an attic entirely too long.

Without moving his legs, the clown was suddenly right in front of the girls, breathing down at them. They ran around him, trying to get to the girl, but the clown followed.

Fed up, Kathy swung her leg and kicked the clown right to the ground. She pressed her foot down against his chest.

"You got the girl?" she called to Samantha.

Before her sister could answer, the clown stood. Kathy's foot slipped, catching on the fabric of his pants and tearing it as he got to its feet. Kathy swung her leg, ready to deliver another kick, when she suddenly felt the ground seem to shift. As if someone were tilting it, like raising up a carpet while she was standing on it.

Disoriented, Kathy fell to the grass, where the ground leveled out, back to normal. She looked up just as the clown disappeared around the corner and out of sight.

CHAPTER 16

Hey!" a woman's voice shouted out.

The man had been so consumed by the little girl's screams that he hadn't sensed anyone arriving. He turned to the sound and saw two women standing at the entry to the room.

At the sight of him, both women gasped, which put a devious smirk on the man's face. He took that opportunity to try to feast some more. The little girl's fears had refueled him enough to gain back a little of his strength, but he needed more. And she wasn't even fully depleted yet. If he hadn't been interrupted...

In an instant, he was in front of the two women, standing uncomfortably close so as to ratchet up their fears. To his surprise, both women avoided his glare and ran around him toward the little girl, who lay screaming and crying in the center of the room.

Once again, the man followed, trying to build up their fears. But something was different about these women. They seemed stronger than most. Most people were more frightened alone than they were with even just one person, but this was different. This was—

It hit him how the two women were different. He sniffed the air to confirm, then his lips turned into a sinister smile.

Witches.

As the women raced to the little girl, he intercepted them. The one in a white sundress swung her leg and kicked him right in the stomach. The move was so unexpected that he stumbled backward onto the ground. Most people were so consumed with terror that they were unable or unwilling to fight back. These women—these witches—were not like any others he had encountered.

Flat on his back, the woman pressed her foot against his chest to pin him there.

"You got the girl?" she asked the other.

The man decided he had had enough. Without straining the body he had created for himself, he rose back to his feet. The woman pinning him got her foot tangled in the fabric of his clothing and it tore.

The woman regained her balance, then spun to deliver

another kick, but the man implemented his own power. To the witch, the ground began to tilt, slanting at an angle that forced her to stumble backward. For everyone else, it looked as if she had suddenly lost her balance and fell.

The man took that opportunity to run off down the opposite pathway from where the witches had arrived. He waited until he was out of view to rescind his second form, disappearing into thin air.

In a matter of seconds, he was back as one being, standing out in the panicking crowd under the day's sun.

"What's going on?" a woman beside him wondered, looking toward the funhouse tent.

"Heard a scream," a man said. "Sounded like a little girl."

"A couple people went in there," someone else said. "Do you think we should call 9-1-1?"

All around him, the man sensed the fear and worry emanating from the crowd. He wished he could feed off of it, but it would blow his cover. Besides, even though he was able to feed off the fears of adults, it was the children he was after. Their fears were much more pure. It reached down to their core, whereas adults tended to suppress their fears and find ways to cope with them.

Luckily, the utter terror that he just consumed from that little girl was enough to sate him for a little bit. But he would need more before he was up to full strength.

Among the crowd, the man spotted the woman who was

supposed to be his wife. She held her daughter tightly in her arms.

"Charles! Charles!" she called to him. "I've got her! Ashley's all right! She's right here!"

The man ran up, hoping he had a believable look of worry on his face, and hugged them. As he pulled away, the little girl looked at him with a wary glance.

Soon, he thought to himself, *I'll feed on you too.*

CHAPTER 17

That was—"

"Scary," Samantha finished for her sister. They were standing outside the tent in the warm sunshine, although their thoughts were still in that dark and confusing funhouse.

Kathy nodded.

"You guys actually *saw* the guy?" Steven whispered.

"Not sure he was a guy," Samantha said, "but yeah. We saw him."

"What did he look like?"

"Like a clown," Kathy said.

"Are you sure he wasn't just someone trying to help that little girl?" he asked.

The trio looked over at the back of the ambulance, where

the first responders were checking in with the little girl, Kelly. She was sitting up and answering questions. Her father, Ned, was sitting right beside her with an arm around her.

Samantha couldn't imagine what the girl—or her father—were going through. As an adult, she was still thinking about what she had just seen in the funhouse. But a kid experiencing that and being the center of that terror? No doubt it would scar her for the rest of her life.

"No, that clown was definitely doing something to her," Samantha said. "He was supernatural in some way."

"At least he ran away when I started to fight back," Kathy said. "I got a piece of his clothing. It ripped off when I kicked him." She fished in her cleavage, where she had stuffed the fabric before leaving the tent, but it wasn't there.

"Kathy, do you mind not feeling yourself up in front of everyone?" Samantha scolded.

"Nobody's looking," Kathy reasoned. "But it's not here."

"Did you lose it?" Steven asked.

"How could she?" Samantha asked sarcastically. "She had it locked up in the most secure place ever."

"I don't have any pockets in this dress, Sam," Kathy snapped back. "It was here, but now it's gone. Actually, now that I think about it, I felt something when they first came in to get Kelly."

"What do you mean?" Steven asked.

"Like the fabric disappeared," Kathy said. "That has to be the only explanation."

"Or…you could've just lost it," Samantha said. "Either way, we don't have it."

"Is that important?" Steven asked.

"We could've used it to track him down," Kathy said. "That's why I kept it."

"We'll have to find another way, then," Samantha said.

Kathy looked over at Kelly and Ned at the back of the ambulance again. She shook her head and turned back to Samantha and Steven. "I just wish I was able to chase him back to wherever he's hiding. It's got to be somewhere in the maze. He didn't come out, did he?"

"Doesn't sound like it," Steven said. "From what I heard, the only ones who left the tent were the ones who ran in after we all heard the scream."

"I should've caught him," Kathy murmured.

"All right, Super Girl," Samantha said. "Take it easy on yourself. Just because you're running now and more athletic doesn't make you invincible. Even if you were to catch up to him in his hiding place, then what would've happened? It would've been the two of you alone on his turf with no idea how to stop him. It's better that we have this chance to regroup."

Kathy nodded her agreement reluctantly.

"And you still saved that little girl," Steven added.

"She's going to have nightmares for the rest of her life, but yeah," Kathy said.

"Nowadays, who isn't a little emotionally scarred?"

Samantha said as an attempt at a joke. When she saw that neither of them even cracked a smile, she added, "I'm sure Kelly's tough. She'll be all right."

"And you're sure that this is something you should be investigating?" Steven asked.

Both girls nodded.

"It definitely is," Samantha said.

"Any idea what you're up against?"

The sisters looked at each other. It had been months since they'd faced anything magical. With all of their other encounters, they typically had a general idea what they were facing. This time, they didn't seem to have enough information yet. All they knew was that the creature they were facing was definitely supernatural, he was quick, and he fed off of fear.

Off the top of her head, Samantha couldn't name anything that fit that description. Judging from her sister's look, Kathy thought the same thing.

"No," Samantha finally said, looking at her husband. "We really don't have a clue what we're facing here."

CHAPTER 18

The man stood at the grill, cooking up all of the hot dogs, hamburgers, and sausage links that they had brought with them. It was pointless, though. Only a fraction of the people remained at the party. Most parents took their kids home, afraid that someone else would snatch them. They were all overreacting. It's not like that little girl was kidnapped or hurt in any way. She was just scared. They were all a bunch of sissies, the man thought.

The woman who was supposed to be his wife had gathered the remaining children and her own little girl around a single picnic table. The pile of wrapped gifts sat in front of the girl, who seemed unsure whether it was okay for her to have fun after what had happened.

Behind the kids, the parents stood nervously. They watched as the girl opened the presents one-by-one with little enthusiasm. Nearly every parent seemed to be glancing over at the funhouse tent every few minutes, their minds elsewhere.

The man's mind was elsewhere too. While he smiled at the girl opening her presents and continued to work the grill, he was also scoping out the reactions of everyone. The two women he saw inside the tent had been making their rounds, talking to anyone who was willing to talk. Parents and various crew members from the carnival. The one was even eyeing up the father of the little girl the man had targeted.

He didn't like it one bit.

Witches were notorious for sticking their noses in where they didn't belong. He was going to have to keep an eye on them to make sure they didn't dig around too much. Even better, he would have to learn as much about them as possible. Maybe put them through their own individualized tricks and tortures.

The man smiled at the thought of that.

CHAPTER 19

The party was subdued after the incident in the funhouse tent. Laurel had been insistent that it continue, although many of the parents had opted to take their kids home. Even with the dwindling party, Charles still manned the grill, cooking enough hamburgers and hot dogs to feed an army. Meanwhile, Laurel gathered the few remaining children with Ashley so the one-year-old could open her gifts.

Samantha wanted to be present at the party, but she also wanted to get as much information as possible about what had happened.

After the police were called, the carnival crew members were on full alert, rushing in and out of the funhouse in search of the clown or any sign of him. Police had also searched nearby tents, but seeing as they were essentially just large rooms, it didn't take long to determine that the perpetrator wasn't hiding in any of them.

Out by the street, Ned and Kelly still sat at the back of the ambulance. The little girl was still too terrified to go home, although the first responders were getting ready to pack up and head back in case they were needed for another call.

With Steven representing them at the party while baby Ashley opened presents, Samantha and Kathy snuck over to the carnival and talked to the crew members. One of them was bound to be chatty and willing to talk about what they knew or didn't know.

"The funhouse is a mystery to all of us too," Travis, one of the crewmen, told the girls. He wore a rolled up flannel shirt and ripped jeans with boots. Samantha couldn't quite figure out how he wasn't sweating to death in the seventy-five degree heat.

"Well, a tent that big must take a lot of people to set up," Kathy said. "Especially with the maze and all the various tricks and gimmicks inside. Who helps?"

"Nah," he said with a crooked smile at her. "You see, what happens is we set up the whole outside of the tent—you know, the awning and sides and stuff—and then Ernest takes over from there."

Travis was the third person they had talked to who had mentioned Ernest as the one responsible for anything to do with the funhouse. He was definitely someone they would need to track down and have a word with. They would need to be careful, though. The police were probably following the same trail of leads.

"He sets up the whole thing by himself?" Samantha asked. "No help at all from anyone?"

"Yeah, pretty much. The funhouse is, like, his brainchild, you know? I guess he proposed it back in the day and he's taken complete control over it. I guess it's pretty popular with the kids, you know what I'm saying? Otherwise the show runners wouldn't let him do it, right?"

"So he sets up by himself in every city?" Samantha asked.

"That's what I said, isn't it? I guess he changes it up every time, too. Not that I've ever been in there. The place freaks me out."

"Freaks you out how?" Samantha asked.

He shook his head. "I don't do clowns, man."

"Why would he change the funhouse in each city?" Kathy asked. "Wouldn't it be easier to keep it the same at every stop?"

"He wants it to be a surprise, I guess." He flashed another crooked smile at her. "You know?"

"What else can you tell us about the funhouse?" Samantha asked. "Any idea what's inside? Does he use the same tricks or does he change those too?"

"Hey lady, I don't know much more than what I've told you." Travis put up his hands as if to surrender. "If you want to know more, you need to talk to Ernest, you know?"

"Any idea where we can find him?" Kathy asked.

Travis bit his bottom lip and pulled up the sleeves of his flannel. "I think he has the day off today, but I could help you search around for him if you'd like."

Samantha moved partially in front of Kathy to get his attention again. "Hi. Wouldn't he be in his trailer? Or would he still be setting up the funhouse?"

Travis sighed and shook his head. "Hey lady, I told you. I think he's off today. And he doesn't have his own trailer. Ma'am, we're essentially roadies. We all bunk together in one trailer. When we get to a city, we take full advantage of the room and board stipend we get."

"So he's staying in a hotel?" Kathy asked.

"Most of us do. There's only a few broke jokes who want to save their money and stay in the trailer all the time."

"Any idea which hotel he's at?" Samantha asked.

Travis shook his head. "No ma'am. We just get a stipend and can choose whatever hotel we want. A lot of places don't like it when a whole crew rolls into town. They think we'll cause too much trouble if we're all in the same place. Disturb the other guests and all that, you know?"

"Have there been disturbances at the hotels?" Samantha asked. She was trying to determine if this clown—Ernest, possibly—was causing a scene in places other than the funhouse tent. If they could follow other instances in other cities, they could use that to further identify what they were up against.

"I mean, we've gotten rowdy in the past, you know?" Travis said with a laugh.

"Rowdy how?" Samantha asked.

"Aw, you know. Partying. Drinking. Having a grand ol' time before we leave town." He looked the older witch up and down. "Well…maybe *you* don't know." He turned to Kathy. "But I'm sure you do."

Samantha raised an eyebrow at the jab, but let it ride. She just wanted him to answer the question and if Kathy could flirt a little to get the information out of him, then that's what they needed to do. At least something good would come from all the attention her sister had been getting today.

"The after show parties," he explained. "Whenever it's the last night in a town and we're leaving the next morning. Traveling all day means we can sleep all day, so we can party all night long."

"And that's why you're encouraged to stay at different hotels," Kathy said with a smirk.

Travis laughed and bit his bottom lip again. "Oh, you know…"

"So nothing weird has happened at the hotel since you've been here?" Samantha pushed. "Or what about in other cities? Has something like this happened before somewhere else?" She nodded her head over to the funhouse tent.

He shook his head. "No. This is the first time something like this has happened. I mean, we get kids screaming and running away scared, but it's just the typical stuff. They're kids. Can't stand something jumping out at them, you know?"

"I thought you've never been inside the funhouse?" Samantha asked.

"Hell no! But I've heard stories."

"Nothing about a little kid being terrorized by a freaky clown?" Kathy asked.

"Nothing like that, but uh, I can get freaky if you want."

Samantha pulled Kathy away. "Okay, I think we've heard enough. Thanks for talking to us."

"Sure thing." He watched them turn and slowly walk back to the party.

Huddled close together as they walked away slowly, Samantha said, "So basically there's no track record of this ever happening before, meaning that we don't have any other clues as to what it is we're facing."

"Yeah, it's too bad Travis couldn't tell us more." She turned and waved to him with a smirk.

Samantha turned her away from Travis. "I know you love the attention, but can you focus?"

"Right. Sorry. So what's our next step?"

Before Samantha could answer, Steven walked up to them. "The party's pretty much breaking up. The presents have all been opened and most of the kids are going home. Did you guys find anything?"

Samantha looked beyond her husband and saw Laurel and

Charles packing up the picnic. The party had been much shorter than Laurel likely intended, but it was probably a good idea to get the kids as far away from the carnival as possible. The last thing they needed was for another incident to occur.

"Not a lot," Kathy said.

"No track record of anything like this happening," Samantha said. "Nothing strange about the funhouse tent, other than the fact that only one guy sets it up every time. And he changes the layout every time."

"That seems a little odd."

She nodded. "That's what we thought too. I'm just concerned about tomorrow. One of the crew members we talked to said they still plan on opening tomorrow for the general public. What if something happens to another kid?"

"We'll have to stop that clown before then," Kathy said.

"Do you even know where to go from here?" Steven asked.

Samantha nodded. "We need to find Ernest. He's the one who sets up the funhouse."

"Any idea where he is?"

She shrugged. "Could be in any hotel in the city."

CHAPTER 20

Ned held his daughter close to his chest as he carried her toward his car, which was parked on the street at the edge of the park. Samantha needed to jog to catch up to him.

"Excuse me!" she called. "Hello! Ned!"

He turned and looked at her. She slowed as she caught up to him, more breathless than she would have liked to admit. As much as she wanted to believe that the pregnancy was to blame, she knew that wasn't true.

"I'm sorry," he said. "I'd really just like to get Kelly home."

"How's she doing?" Samantha asked. She had seen them start to leave from across the park and wanted to talk to them before they left. If anyone would have the most information about what they were up against, it was one of the clown's victims.

Ned cradled his daughter's head in his hand as she nuzzled close to his neck. "She's terrified. What do you think?"

Samantha sighed. "I know. And I'm sorry for being intrusive. I just want to do what I can to help stop whoever it was that was in there. My sister and I were the two who found her."

"Oh." His demeanor turned less hostile. "Well, thanks."

"You're welcome." Samantha offered a genuine smile. "Has she said anything about what she's seen?"

Kelly began to stir in his arms and let out a whimper.

"Do you mind walking with me to my car?" he asked. "I want to put her down. She's been through enough today."

"Of course."

They walked down to a black pick-up truck parked in the last spot on West 8th Street. Samantha stood back as Ned opened the door, climbed up and eased Kelly into the booster seat in the back.

After several minutes, Kelly was successfully buckled into her seat. Ned climbed out of the truck and leaned against it, leaving the passenger door open.

"It's hotter than hell in there, but she's so cold," he said with a sigh. "Her skin is like ice. I'm just trying to warm her up. She's still so terrified."

"She's cold to the touch?"

He nodded. "And her heart is racing. The paramedics said

it's not at a level that's concerning, but it's still faster than normal."

"Are you going to take her to a doctor?"

"They didn't seem to think she needed to." He shrugged. "I don't know. I guess I'll just take her home and see if I can get her to calm down in a place she feels comfortable."

"That sounds like a good idea."

Ned wiped his hand over his face and Samantha wondered if he was on the edge of tears. He shook away any pending emotion and said, "I'm sorry. You wanted to figure out what happened."

"Did Kelly say anything about what she saw in the tent?"

"Just that she saw a clown and thought he was part of the funhouse. He *should* have been part of the funhouse. Apparently you can't trust anyone anymore."

"No, you can't." Samantha couldn't help but reach for her own belly and worry about the safety of her unborn child. She hoped she was never in the same shoes as Ned was, but her lifestyle wasn't always safe.

"It was just so weird. She was laughing and smiling one minute, then I took my eyes off of her for *one second* so I could get us some drinks and she was gone. When she came out of that tent, she was shaking. Utterly terrified." He looked down and shook his head, blinking repeatedly.

Samantha looked away to give him a bit of privacy with his emotion.

"Anyway," he said with a heavy tone. "I should get her home. I'm sorry we don't know much more, but I appreciate you finding her. Hopefully you can find the bastard who was in there with her. I can't believe he just disappeared. He's gotta be somewhere around here. Maybe even watching us and getting his jollies by seeing how scared she was."

That thought had crossed Samantha's mind, but finding information about the attack was more important than finding someone hiding in the crowd.

"Do you have something to write with?" she asked. "I want to give you my number. If Kelly remembers anything—or if anything else strange happens to her—give me a call. My name's Samantha."

He reached in his glove compartment and produced a small pad of paper and a pen.

She jotted down her number and passed it back to him. "Like I said, don't hesitate to call. And if you can't reach me, leave a message. I'll get back to you as soon as I can."

"Thank you," he said. "I really hope that you can figure out who's behind this. It takes a sick person to hide in a tent and scare kids."

CHAPTER 21

"Did he have anything good to say?" Kathy asked when Samantha returned to her and Steven.

The older sister shook her head. "That little girl is shaken right to the core. Heart racing, afraid to let go of her father, cold to the touch."

"Cold to the touch?" Steven asked. "That's not normal, is it?"

Samantha shrugged. "We have no idea what we're facing, so I have no idea what's normal and what isn't."

"Which is why we need to get home and check the magic book," Kathy said. "The sooner we know what we're facing, the sooner we can come up with a plan to stop whatever it is that did that to her."

"Good," Steven said. "This party's pretty much dead anyway."

"Actually," Samantha said, "I don't think it's a good idea for us all to leave right away."

"How come?" he asked.

"Well, it's a public park," Samantha started. "Sure, the carnival was only open for Laurel's party, but the funhouse tent is already set up. Kelly snuck in when her father wasn't looking. Who's to say that some other kid wouldn't do the same?"

"You want one of us to stay back and guard the funhouse tent," Kathy said.

Samantha nodded. "Right."

"What about the police?" Steven asked. "Aren't they going to patrol it to make sure nobody goes in?"

"There wasn't really a crime, according to them," Samantha said. "A little girl got scared. Sure, Kathy and I know that he's a paranormal creep who needs to be stopped, but from the police perspective, it's not like the girl was harmed in any physical way."

"So we're on our own," Kathy said.

"Right," Samantha said. "And the carnival is not going to want to close down the funhouse because then they'll lose business and create a reputation that the carnival is unsafe. Plus, again, from everyone else's perspective, a little girl just got scared."

"So basically we need to guard the tent ourselves," Kathy said.

"I don't agree." Steven shook his head. "After what happened earlier, nobody would want to go in there."

"Or would they?" Kathy asked. "As a kid, if I knew that something freaky happened somewhere, I would want to check it out for myself. The fact that Kelly was attacked might be the incentive to make a kid—some teenager, probably—want to go in there. Even if they hadn't thought about it before."

"And we don't know if this clown creep has a preference for younger kids or if Kelly was just in the wrong place at the wrong time," Samantha added. "Either way, I don't want to take any chances."

"Okay. So who's going to stay behind?" he asked.

"Well…" Samantha said with a cringe. "Kathy and I need to check the book and discuss what we're facing. We might even need to come up with a spell or a potion or something to stop them before we regroup."

"And we still need to find that Ernest guy," Kathy added. "He's the one who knows all the secrets to the funhouse."

"So," Steven said, "what you're saying is—"

Samantha flashed a bright smile at her husband. "I need you to do me a *huge* favor."

CHAPTER 22

The sisters sat in Kathy's bedroom with *The Art of Magic*, their family magic book, spread out on the bed. Kathy laid back against the headboard while Samantha sat on the hardwood and leaned her arms on the edge of the bed, absently flipping through pages.

"Well, we've been through the whole thing twice," Kathy said. "We can't find any kind of magical being that feeds on children's fear."

Samantha continued flipping through the pages. "Then we must have something wrong. Maybe it wasn't her fear he was feeding on, but her youth?"

"If that were the case, wouldn't Kelly be dead? Or close to it? Maybe even look like a little old lady at—how old is she? Five? Six?"

"But we interrupted him," Samantha said, continuing to search the book. "Maybe he didn't have a chance to really get started."

"Then how do you explain the clown getup?"

"If he feeds off children's youth, maybe that's how he lures them to him."

"What kid nowadays do you know of that actually likes clowns and will approach one of their own free will?" Kathy asked. "If he wanted access to kids, there are other ways to falsely gain a kid's trust."

"Then maybe he was doing something else to her."

"Maybe we need to consult something other than our magic book."

For the first time, Samantha looked up at her sister. "What do you mean? What else is there?"

"Well, think of the valkyries."

Samantha scrunched her brows together. "I'm not following."

"They existed, but until they took me away to Valhalla, there wasn't much in our magic book about them," Kathy explained. "Because until you and I got an inside scoop into that mythical world, nobody else in our family knew enough about them to write about them in our family magic book."

"So you're saying we might be facing something nobody has ever encountered before?"

"At least nobody who has used our magic book as a resource."

Pulling away from the book, Samantha sat cross-legged on

the floor and tucked her hair behind her ears before she asked, "Okay, so, in general, what do you think we're looking at here? Something from mythology?"

Kathy shrugged. "It's possible. That's definitely a lead we can follow. I wouldn't be surprised to learn about creatures that exist in mythology that feed off of children's fear—if that's what we're assuming."

"I think that's all we can assume," Samantha said. "Kelly's father said she was absolutely terrified. And from what we saw, it's not like the clown was outwardly scaring her. I'm sure the whole situation made her afraid once she realized she was in trouble, but all he was really doing was standing over her and…pulling some kind of energy from her."

"Yeah. Makes me wonder what would've happened to her if you and I hadn't stopped him."

Samantha shook her head. "I don't want to think about that. What we need to do, though, is find out who that clown really is and how to stop him."

"Before he has a chance to hurt anyone else."

"Right." Samantha checked the clock radio beside Kathy's bed. It was going on five o'clock. "I don't think we really have time to go to the library and sift through an endless amount of mythology textbooks. And 'someone that feeds on fear' isn't something we can find in a book's index."

"We could ask someone."

"Oh, sure, let's just ask someone a question about a

supernatural being. And expect them to have an encyclopedic knowledge of everything mythological."

Kathy waved her finger. "Actually, last semester my one English professor seemed very knowledgable about mythology. I could go ask him."

"That's a good idea!"

Kathy checked the time. "I'd have to leave now and hope I catch him before the Memorial Day weekend."

"Actually, now that you mention it, I think I had a professor my first year at Gannon that taught a mythology course. I took his English 200 class, but his mythology class was an elective I considered until I'd realized that I had packed my schedule with accounting classes."

Kathy rolled her eyes with a smirk. "Accounting sounds like a terribly boring major."

"Anyway," Samantha said loudly to brush off her sister's jab, "we could split up and ask both of them. It's a good thing we both cars here. I'll take Steven's and you take mine. We'll meet back here when we're done and figure out what to do next."

"Hopefully we can catch them before they leave—" Kathy was interrupted when she heard the phone ringing downstairs.

"That could be Steven, calling from a payphone," Samantha said.

The sisters looked at each other for a couple seconds before they both jumped up and raced down the stairs to answer the phone.

CHAPTER 23

Kathy was the first to reach the phone in the kitchen. She was a little breathless when she said, "Hello?"

She didn't immediately hear a voice on the other end. Instead, she heard the muffled sound of a crowd, along with glasses clanging and the murmured sound of a television playing.

Finally, she heard Michael's voice come on the line. "Kathy?"

"Michael?" She was surprised that Jeremy's friend and roommate was calling her. "What's going on?"

"I need your help."

Samantha walked in and Kathy furrowed her brow, trying to communicate with her while on the phone. "I'm kind of pressed for time."

"I found Jeremy at the Irish Cousins…again," Michael told her.

"The Irish…" Kathy began before she remembered that the Irish Cousins was a bar on Main Street in Lawrence Park. It was just around the corner from Jeremy and Michael's apartment. "What do you mean 'again'?"

"Your boyfriend is currently wasted," he said plainly. "Just like he's been the last several times I've found him here. It's been a couple weeks already. The problem is, this time he refuses to leave with me."

Kathy's head was spinning. She brought a hand to her forehead and leaned against the stair banister. "Wait, wait, wait. You're saying he's been going there every week?"

"At least once a week, sometimes twice a week," Michael said. "I've usually been able to drag him out of here myself but today he's refusing. I thought that maybe you would be able to talk some sense into him."

She had no idea that Jeremy was doing this. Whenever she saw him, he seemed like his normal self. Granted, with her evening work schedule and the final weeks of the semester, she had really only seen him on Sundays or Mondays. Still, she thought she would've heard something about this. Even when they couldn't see each other, they talked on the phone often enough.

"Um…" Kathy looked over at her sister, who watched her curiously. "I guess I'll be right there. Give me about twenty-five, thirty minutes."

"I'll try to keep him in check until then," Michael said.

"Thanks Kathy. And sorry for dumping this on you. I thought you knew."

"No, I didn't." She moved her hair out of her face, feeling her body tighten with stress. "I'll see you soon."

"What was that about?" Samantha asked when Kathy had hung up. She already had Steven's car keys in her hand.

Kathy debated not telling her sister about Jeremy, but was so blown away by the news that she needed to tell someone. And, if she was being honest, she was pissed that this was the first time she was hearing about this. Jeremy had always liked to drink, but never to the extent of getting drunk every week by himself. She thought he was growing up and growing out of that phase in his life.

Guess she thought wrong.

"That was Michael." Kathy reached for Samantha's keys. "Jeremy's drunk and he needs my help getting him home." She braced for a lecture, but was surprised when it never came.

"Where?"

"Lawrence Park," Kathy said. "Hopefully he walked down there so he's not tempted to drive home. Do you mind if I still take your car?"

"No, that's fine," Samantha said. "Are you okay?"

"I don't really have time to worry about this." Kathy led her sister to the front door. "We need to figure out what attacked Kelly, which means you need to catch that professor before he leaves for the weekend. I'm sorry, but I guess you're on your own."

Samantha nodded. "It's not your fault. Hopefully he can tell me what we want to know."

"Yeah. I have no idea how long I'll be or if I'll even be home at all tonight."

"That's okay," Samantha said. "I'll figure it out and we can regroup later. The biggest thing is keeping anyone out of that funhouse tent and figuring out how to stop this creep before he finds someone else. You take care of Jeremy."

"Thanks."

Samantha gave her sister a quick hug. "We'll get through this."

The younger sister hugged her back, realizing just how much she was shaken by the news now that she finally had some comfort.

"I'm going to grab some overnight clothes real quick and then I'm going to leave," Kathy said. "You should go now. You don't want to miss him."

"Okay. Call me if you need my help later."

"Will do."

Samantha left and Kathy went upstairs to pack a quick overnight bag. When she and Jeremy first dated, she had kept a few clothes at his house. Now, however, between work and school she didn't spend as many nights at Jeremy's apartment as she used to so she didn't have a drawer full of clothes in his dresser.

She packed shorts and a T-shirt to sleep in, fresh socks and underwear, and a change of clothes for the next day. She had a feeling she was going to be spending the night with Jeremy, insisting he drink water and helping him to the bathroom to make sure he vomited in the toilet and not all over his room.

These were things she had done when he went through his party phase in college. She thought those days were behind them. How easily they seemed to slip back into those roles.

Just before she left her bedroom, she decided to throw her running shoes and some exercise clothes in the bag as well. She already felt so tense with stress that she knew a run would help her relax. If she wasn't so pressed for time, she would've ran right out of the house and kept running until she felt better. Too bad that wasn't an option.

Back downstairs, Kathy raced through the foyer and toward the front door when she heard the phone ring again. She debated letting the machine get it, but thought it might be Michael telling her that Jeremy had decided to go home on his own and she wasn't needed. Then, at least, she could go see if that professor was still at Porecco and get some information on what might've been hiding in that funhouse. She could deal with Jeremy later.

"Hello?" Kathy said in the kitchen when she picked up the phone.

"Kathleen Walker?"

"Speaking."

"Hi! It's Darlene Napier at Porecco College. I hope I'm not calling too late?"

"Actually, I'm—"

"I just wanted to give you a call because I see in our system that it says your major is still undeclared? Is that correct? Did I miss a form somewhere?"

Kathy couldn't believe she was dealing with this in addition to everything else the day had thrown at her. "Yeah, I—"

"Have you decided on a major?"

"No, I haven't."

"Well, you really need to make your declaration so we can better steer your education toward your goals," Darlene said. "If you don't, we may ask you to—"

"I'm dropping out," Kathy said abruptly. It was something she had considered before. At that moment, though, with everything else stretching her too thin, she had had enough and wanted to unload something from her to-do list. College wasn't making her happy. In fact, she thought that she had become more unhappy since she began taking classes last fall.

"Oh." Darlene was startled. "Can I ask why?"

"I'm just too busy," Kathy said. "In fact, I need to go right now. So if you need me to do any paperwork to properly drop out, please mail it to me. Otherwise, I have to go." She hung up before Darlene could say anything else.

As she raced out the door and fired up Samantha's car, Kathy felt a little relief that one chapter of her life was over. As she backed onto the street to put out one fire in her life while another one was burning elsewhere, Kathy couldn't help but smile.

This would be the start to something good.

CHAPTER 24

The halls of the Palumbo Academic Center at Gannon University were empty when Samantha arrived. Worried that she might miss Professor Gray, she ignored the nostalgic feeling she felt when she stepped through the doors for the first time in over a year.

Moving up to the third floor, Samantha located the English department office suite and stepped in. Most of the desks had been vacated for the long weekend. Only two professors remained, neither of which were Professor Gray.

"Damn," Samantha murmured to herself.

One of the professors looked up at her. "Can I help you with something?"

"Is Professor—" Her question was cut short as the door

behind her opened, nearly colliding into her. Stepping through was the familiar face she had been looking for. Dressed in a short-sleeved button-up shirt and a yellow tie that had been pulled loose, Professor Gray was a portly man with a receding graying hairline and glasses that hung on the edge of his large nose.

"Oh, hello," he said with a polite smile.

"Professor Gray?"

He looked at her with uncertainty, likely trying to decide if she was one of his students.

"My name's Samantha Harper," she said. "I was in your English class about five years ago."

His eyes widened as he stepped over to his desk and began collecting his papers into his briefcase. "Forgive me if I don't remember you specifically. I've had a lot of students since then."

"Of course, yeah," she said. "And my name's changed too. It used to be Walker."

Professor Gray shook his head, indicating that the name didn't register any recollection.

"Anyway," she said, "I was hoping you'd be able to answer some questions I had. You see, I'm working on this short story and I want to make sure I get the mythology right."

His eyebrows lifted. "A short story? How admirable. Unfortunately, you've caught me on my way out. Perhaps we can schedule a time to meet next week? I'm teaching two summer courses, but I could always squeeze out some time to talk mythology."

"Would it be too much trouble to talk now?" Samantha's eyes flickered over to the two other professors who were in the office. She didn't want them to overhear their discussion—too many other people to speculate that she wasn't being truthful about the short story tale she told.

He snapped his briefcase closed and grabbed ahold of the handle. "Actually, I'm in a bit of a hurry. My wife is waiting for me to come home. We're spending the weekend camping in the Allegheny Forest."

"I could follow you out to your car and we can walk and talk, if that's okay."

He sighed, then checked his watch. "I admire your persistence. Yes, I suppose that would be all right. Come now. As I said, my wife is waiting."

They left the office and headed for the staircase that would lead them to the second floor, where the entrance to the attached parking garage was located.

"You see, I want to write a bit of a scary story," she started. "Something that'll draw on people's inner fears. My main villain is someone who feeds off of the fear of his victims."

"Intriguing."

They descended the stairs and rounded the corner down the hall toward the door to the parking garage.

"Yeah, and I want to reveal that this villain is actually a

mythological creature, but I'm not sure what creature would fit the bill."

"What mythology are you looking at specifically? Greek? Roman?"

"Any," she said. "I'm open to them all."

"Well, there's attachment spirits from Native American and Eastern European mythologies," he said. "Although you'd have to add into your story a scene where they latch on to a person and use them as a host."

Samantha made a face. "I'm not thinking about possession here."

"It's not quite possession," he clarified. "They're attaching themselves to people, feeding off of their fears to keep control over them."

"What else is there?" she asked.

They pushed through the doors into the parking garage and walked along the short row of cars. Being that there was only summer classes, the parking garage wasn't nearly as full as it usually was during a regular semester.

"There's also a succubus, who can be manipulative—or the male counterpart, incubus."

"Aren't those the, um, *sexual* ones?"

He nodded. "Well, yes. Again, you'd have to add that part into your story."

"The victims are children," she said, then remembered the lie she was hiding behind. "And the symbolism with one of the characters is strong and I don't want to get rid of that."

"Ah, I see. Yes, then a succubus wouldn't work." He stopped at a red sedan and placed his briefcase on it possessively, but showed no sign of cutting their conversation short. "Well, you might consider a demonology mythology. I don't remember off the top of my head, but you could look into demons that may gain energy by feeding off of the fears of children. Perhaps they possessed someone who is doing the bidding for them."

She shook her head. "I don't really want to go down the possession route." *Although*, she wondered, *maybe that clown is actually a demon.*

Professor Gray shook his head. "It sounds like your story needs more substance before you can settle on a particular creature."

"What do you mean?"

"Well, some other clue that would lead to a more likely being," he explained. "For instance, if something were going on in the background that isn't noticeable at first until the main character discovers there's a connection to the being."

"You mean like something going on in the environment when the being is around?" She tried to think back to the park and pinpoint anything in the weather that was happening, but it was a bright, sun-filled day. The only oddity was that the funhouse tent felt cold and gloomy when they were inside.

"Not necessarily limited to nature," he said. "It could be anything. For example, misplaced keys or knotted laces on sneakers might indicate an imp or some other mischievous creature is lurking. Or take, for instance, a trickster. If anything strange were happening in the area of where your victims were attacked, that would indicate that a trickster were at play."

"What do you mean by strange? I've never heard of a trickster."

"Most cultures have some version of a trickster in their mythologies," he explained. "The most notable, perhaps, is Loki, in Norse mythology. But there are others as well. Tricksters can alter reality, distort things, cause disruption and chaos, those sorts of things."

Samantha knew firsthand that Loki was still locked up by Odin. If he wasn't, she knew the valkyries would've unleashed their army by now.

"You mean, like, break a perfectly good lawn chair, make a can of pop explode in someone's face, and create a random gust of wind?" The memories of that afternoon's party were coming back. The smaller things that had been overshadowed in her mind after the incident with Kelly.

"Exactly! Add those details to your story and revealing the trickster as the villain would be perfectly logical."

"But do tricksters feed off the fear of children?"

"It depends on the mythology you're pulling your information from," he said. "Some cultures believe that tricksters were just having fun. Others believed that tricksters intentionally scared people to feed off their fear and survive.

Maybe yours has just decided to target children."

"Maybe," she murmured. It sounds like the most plausible option. "Any idea how to stop them?"

"*Stop* them?" He shook his head. "They're usually gods, Mrs. Harper. They can't typically be stopped. Only contained."

She gave him a tight smile. "You're right. I won't keep you any longer. Thanks for the help."

"Of course. Good luck with your story. I look forward to reading it."

Samantha promised to send him a copy of the story she had no intention of writing. Meanwhile, her mind raced with her next steps forward. She didn't believe that the trickster couldn't be stopped. There was a way to stop everyone. And she was determined to find it.

CHAPTER 25

The Irish Cousins sat on the corner of Main Street and Rankine Avenue in Lawrence Park. Kathy managed to find parking on Rankine, right near the door. That way, she wouldn't have to drag Jeremy very far once she finally got him out of the bar. She was grateful that she didn't see his car anywhere nearby. At least he hadn't driven himself.

As soon as she stepped through the door, Michael walked over to greet her. Behind him, she saw her boyfriend curled over the bar, twirling his finger over the rim of his glass.

"Thanks for coming." Michael took her arm and led her to a spot beside the jukebox away from the door. "He's not in great shape."

"Has he at least stopped drinking?" she asked.

"The bartender stopped serving him right before I called. He's taking his time with his last drink."

"Well, there's something."

"Has he mentioned anything to you about being depressed?"

"Michael, this is the first I'm hearing about any of this," she said with an edge to her voice. "No, he hasn't said anything. Why?"

"He's been talking about how he hates his job. I think that's what's fueling this drunken bender."

"You don't become an alcoholic just because you hate your job," she said. In her mind, she faintly recalled a conversation where Jeremy indicated that he didn't love his job and that it was only a way to pay the bills. Of course, she was kicking herself for brushing that comment under the table by feeling sorry for herself that she didn't even have any kind of full-time job.

"You think he's an alcoholic?"

"I don't know what to think right now!" she snapped. "All I want to do is get him home and get him sober."

Kathy knew that Michael didn't deserve her disrespect, but he was the only one she could take her anger out on at the moment.

She approached Jeremy, but before she could reach him he noticed her and shouted, "Kathy!"

Everyone in the bar looked up at her and she just wanted to disappear.

"Keep your voice down," she hissed at him. "What is this? What are you doing? And why haven't you told me you've been coming here?" She could hear Michael walk up behind her.

"I don't have to tell you anything," Jeremy slurred. "We're not married. You don't *own* me! If I want to get—" He looked over at a group of guys down the bar and pointed at Kathy. "Hey fellas. D'you believe this? She thinks she can boss me around! I haven't put a ring on it! I don't need to answer to some bitch."

Kathy bit her top lip and reached for his arm, letting her anger out by squeezing him hard.

"Ow!" he shouted. "You're not getting a ring if you *abuse* me like that!"

"I'm taking you home," she said.

"The hell you are!"

"Jeremy, buddy, come on," Michael said.

Jeremy looked between the two of them. "Are you two sleeping together? Is that what this is?"

"No, what this is are two people who care about you and want you to get your sorry ass into bed before you make a bigger fool of yourself," Kathy said. "Now get up and get out to my car so I can get you to bed."

"You going to put me to bed, Mommy?"

"If you're going to act like a child, then I'll treat you like one." She could feel all the eyes in the room watching them as Jeremy continued to make a scene.

She just wanted to get out of there.

She just wanted to get away from Jeremy.

Michael grabbed Jeremy's other arm and lifted him to his feet.

"Hey! Let me go!" Jeremy shouted. "Abuse! Someone call the cops! These guys are manhandling me!"

Luckily, everyone at the bar just watched without saying a word. Kathy struggled to get Jeremy's arm around her shoulders as Michael did the same on the other side. Together, they grabbed around his waist and dragged him out onto the sidewalk.

They made it to Samantha's car before Jeremy bent over and vomited right beside it.

"You've *got* to be kidding me," Kathy murmured.

Jeremy sunk to the ground, away from the pile he just spewed. "I'm okay! I'm okay. I'm just going to take a quick nap. Right here."

Enraged, Kathy put her hands on her hips and watched him fall to the ground. Michael struggled to keep his friend from sinking any lower.

"Jeremy, get up," Kathy demanded.

Yanking on his arm, Michael managed to get Jeremy back onto his feet.

Kathy opened the door and Jeremy slumped inside.

"If you puke all over my sister's car, I'll knock you out and then revive you so she can take a shot herself," Kathy threatened. "Got it?"

Jeremy gave her a thumbs up and she shut the door on him.

"I'm going to follow you back to our place," Michael said. "I can help you get him inside, but then I have to go. Maddie and I have dinner plans and things haven't been great between us, so I can't miss it."

Kathy rubbed her face, then pulled her hair back. She quickly tied it on the top of her head, needing one less thing to worry about at that moment.

"That's okay," she said. "Thanks for calling me. And thanks for helping."

"No problem. I just wish I could help you with the detox. And the inevitable discussion that's going to come up between you two."

"Oh joy. As if I don't have enough to worry about."

"Do you want me to cancel my dinner?"

She shook her head. "No. You go and take a break. Sounds like you've been fighting this battle for weeks. Now it's my turn."

To her surprise, Michael reached down and gave her a hug. It felt nice to finally be comforted in some way. "Call me if you need any help. Maddie's number is on the fridge at the apartment."

She pulled away from him and smiled. "Thanks."

Michael wandered off to his car and Kathy went around to the driver's seat. Jeremy had already fallen asleep. She turned the key in the ignition, signaled, and pulled away from the curb.

Meanwhile, her thoughts were swimming with Jeremy. How long had this been going on for? And if he kept this a secret, what other secrets was he keeping from her?

CHAPTER 26

Samantha sat hunched over a book at the library. Several other books lay open on the table around her. There was a stack of discarded books piled up in the corner that she had already gone through.

The place was silent. The sun had set, signaling the late hour.

In the corner of the room, Steven sat impatiently in a comfortable chair. He was already halfway through a Clive Cussler book. Samantha had never seen him read before, but apparently he was fresh out of options to keep him entertained.

She had picked him up from the park after meeting with Professor Gray, but she wanted to rush right to the library to look further into tricksters before the library closed. They had already been here for an hour and until she found a way to stop a trickster—or the library staff kicked her out—she had no intention of leaving.

So far, out of all the textbooks and encyclopedias that she had collected, she had only found a few scant references to tricksters. Most of the texts indicated Loki, Anansi, or Velds, among others, as notable tricksters.

What was difficult, however, was that nearly every cultural mythology she looked at had a trickster entity of some sort, just as Professor Gray had indicated. Some books mentioned ways that ancient gods stopped the tricksters from their chaos, but so far nothing was within her abilities.

"Are you almost done yet?" Steven asked from across the room.

"I'm still looking for a way to stop this trickster."

"And how long will that take?"

"As long as it does, Steven." She let out a deep breath and added, "I don't know how long."

He huffed and turned back to his book. "Didn't think I'd be spending my whole day off sitting around doing nothing."

"You know, you could help me," she said. "It'd get done a lot faster."

"I don't know what I'm looking for!"

"A way to stop a trickster. Something that we can actually do."

Steven made a big show of finding something to use as a

bookmark and stuffing it between the pages. He sauntered over to the table, dropping his book down with a thud, and sat across from his wife. "What am I looking for?"

Samantha pointed to the pile of books in the corner. "Those are the ones that don't even mention tricksters, so they can be returned." She moved to several opened books beside her. "These talk about tricksters in general. I haven't had a chance to really look through the indexes to see if they mention anything else. You could start there. Right now, I'm working on seeing if we could try any of the ways that specific tricksters have been stopped."

"I take it you haven't had any luck?"

She shook her head. "A lot of these textbooks just mention Loki. He's kind of the most famous one, I guess. But we can rule him out."

"How come?"

"Kathy and I took that trip to Valhalla last summer, remember?"

Steven's eyebrows raised. "Man, that was almost a year ago now."

"It's coming up to it."

Samantha returned to her book. She didn't want to read anymore about snake venom keeping Loki in place. She didn't want to read about mythical imprisonments. She wanted a tried-and-true mortal-tested way to stop a trickster.

And then she found it.

Located in a photo caption opposite the trickster entry read: *"Some tales tell of warriors stopping tricksters in a similar way that they might stop a shapeshifter: a wooden stake to the heart, dipped in the blood of one of the trickster's previous victims."*

Samantha smiled. *That* she could do. All she needed to do now was somehow dip a wooden stake in Kelly's blood.

Yeah, like *that* wouldn't be an issue.

CHAPTER 27

Kathy returned to Jeremy's house from her morning jog. It had helped her relieve some stress from the night before. But she was still annoyed by the whole situation and she felt guilty for ditching Samantha when they had the trickster to deal with.

After having a glass of water herself, she poured a glass for Jeremy and carried it into his bedroom. She had made it a point to sleep on the couch in the living room, not that he probably noticed.

When she walked in the room, Jeremy began to stir. She hadn't bothered to close any of the curtains when she and Michael had dumped him in bed the night before. The most she had done was take off his shoes.

"Morning," she said a little louder than necessary. "You need to drink more water."

Jeremy squinted at her and sat up. He reached out and took the glass from her and drank the whole thing down.

"Thanks." His voice sounded croaky, like a frog. This was probably his first sip of water in almost twelve hours.

Kathy took a seat on the edge of his bed and looked around at the small room. Being back here reminded her of her whole turbulent relationship with Jeremy. This room had both been a refuge and a battlefield.

And it wasn't anything special.

While she had only recently thought of Jeremy as more mature and someone who was getting his life together, his bedroom still looked like it belonged to a sloppy teenager. There were piles of dirty clothes, bags of chips and other snacks stashed in the corner, and an overflowing garbage can on the opposite side of his bed. The room generally had a funky smell that she didn't miss at all.

Had either of them really changed all that much? Jeremy still lived like a spoiled brat and Kathy had just dropped out of school on a whim. When were they going to grow up? Was this second shot at their relationship any different from the first?

But it *had* been different. They both worked now. They saw each other for dinner occasionally. Sometimes Jeremy spent the night at her house, but not often. Only once since they had gotten back together had Kathy spent the night at Jeremy's house. And then last night.

"So it sounds like we have some things to talk about," Kathy started.

He made a face, refusing to shake his head. "Not now."

"I think now's the perfect time. What's this business about you hating your job?"

Jeremy ran a hand through his matted hair, then rubbed the sleep out of his eyes. "I'm bored. I want to quit."

"You can't quit until you find something else."

"Don't you think I know that? Don't you think that's just making me feel worse? I feel stuck, Kathy. You wouldn't understand."

She scoffed. "You don't think I get it? Trust me, I know exactly how it feels to hate a job but still be dependent on it. And honestly, I shouldn't even have to tell you this because you should know."

"Kind of like you should've known that I hated my job," he said. "I *told* you that. Several times."

"You haven't made any effort to find anything else, though, have you? So instead, you decided to take the easy way out and wallow in your self-pity. Get *drunk*, like you've always done."

Jeremy turned away from her. "I didn't even want Michael to call you last night."

"Oh, you remember that? Trust me, you made it perfectly clear last night when you embarrassed me in front of the whole bar. You were a mess, Jeremy. And I don't want to ever have to drag you out of a place like that again!"

"Yeah, well, maybe you won't have to."

She opened her mouth to ask what he meant by that, but the phone began to ring in the next room. She started to get up to answer it, but they heard Michael get it before she could leave the room.

How long had he been out there? How much of their argument did he hear?

"Hello? Hi Samantha. Yeah, she's here. I'll get her."

Kathy and Jeremy could hear every word of the conversation on the other side of the door. So it was likely that Michael had heard their whole argument.

There was a soft knock on the doorframe and Michael stuck his head in. "Kathy, your sister's on the phone."

She looked at him and offered a sad smile. In a small voice, she said, "Thanks. I'll be right there."

He disappeared back into the kitchen.

Turning to Jeremy, Kathy said, "I need to go home. I have things to do."

Are you going to be okay by yourself?

The question was on the tip of her tongue, but she couldn't bring herself to ask it. She cared about him and wanted him to get better, but she was not going to be his crutch through a problem that he had created for himself. She had too much work to do on herself before she could be any kind of support for anyone else.

"Fine then. Go."

Kathy stood and made it to the door. She looked back at Jeremy, but he refused to look at her.

Maybe, she thought to herself, *his silence is telling me all I need to know.*

CHAPTER 28

The crew workers for the carnival were already setting up for the day when Samantha and Kathy arrived at Frontier Park. Both sisters moved with purpose toward the funhouse tent. Kathy especially wanted to make up for the time they had lost when she had to go pull her drunken boyfriend out of the bar. She was still seething from that experience.

Crew members worked all over the carnival grounds. They were moving in and out of tents, setting up midway games, rolling out trash cans and picnic tables. The whole place had a buzz about it that hadn't seemed to be there the day before. Apparently Laurel's pretty penny only got her so much. She would have to come to the actual show if she wanted the best experience.

The funhouse tent was open, but the sisters didn't dare go in. Instead, Samantha flagged down one of the crew members as he walked by with a toolbox in his hand.

"Excuse me," she said. It wasn't until he turned around that she recognized him as Travis, who they had talked to the day before. "Oh. Hi."

"Well, hello again." Travis smiled and took a step toward Kathy before backing off.

Samantha glanced over at her sister, who crossed her arms and gave him a "try me" look.

"Do you know where Ernest is?" Samantha asked.

Travis rubbed the back of his head. "Um. He should be in the funhouse. If not, he's down at catering getting some breakfast."

"Where's catering?"

Travis pointed. "In the back of the field, by that path there."

Samantha followed where he was pointing and saw a plain white tent tucked away behind trailers. Clearly, it was not meant for the general public.

"Okay, thanks."

They turned, but Travis reached for Kathy, who swung her arm around and snatched his wrist.

"There's nothing between us," she snapped. "Let it go."

"Whoa, sorry lady!" Travis's face displayed his nerves about having crossed a line.

The two of them stared at each other before Kathy released

him and walked on with Samantha.

"That was…"

"I know," Kathy said. "But I couldn't help it. I'm not in the mood to be schmoozed. I've been taken advantage of too much already."

"How's Jeremy?" Samantha navigated them around the tents of the carnival, toward the trailers that carried equipment and crew members.

"Hung over, as he should be. Apparently he's depressed. Hates his job. Wants to quit. Didn't like it when I told him he needed to stick it out until something better came."

"Maybe he just wants someone to commiserate with."

Kathy glared at her sister. "Don't defend him."

"I'm not. I'm just trying to see it from all sides. I have to be honest, though, Kathy. This whole thing with the drinking kind of scares me a little."

The younger sister rolled her eyes. "It's fine, Sam."

"No, it's not. He's—what? Twenty-three? Twenty-four? He's always been a bit of a partier, but now he's not in college anymore. It's not cute or funny or redeeming in any sense. Yet he still drinks. If he's already developing a drinking problem, that's going to follow him for his entire life. Do you really want to deal with that your whole life?"

"It's not really up to me, though, is it? It's his decision to stop drinking and fix his life. Besides, he's slowed down considerably now that he has a job, if you don't count these last few weeks.

He'll get his act together sooner than later."

"I'm just saying," Samantha pushed. "Tread carefully."

"Yeah, yeah." Kathy stepped behind the tent flap into catering. The whole place smelled like greasy breakfast sausage and hash browns, which reminded Kathy that the only thing she had had for breakfast was a ripe banana at Jeremy's house.

She turned to the person standing at the end of the catering line. "Can you tell us where Ernest is?"

The crew member looked out among the small grouping of tables and pointed to an old man sitting by himself in the corner. The sisters offered thanks to the crew member and then made their way over, each of them sitting beside him.

"Well, hello Ernest," Kathy said.

He looked up. He had longer gray hair, some of which was braided that hung down onto his shoulders. His face was covered in wrinkles, likely from overexposure to the sun over the years as he was very tan. He had a tiny build, although he seemed to move with a youthfulness even some people the sisters' age would envy.

"He-hello," he stuttered when they sat down. "This area is supposed to be for crew members only."

"We won't be here long," Kathy said. "Actually, we were going to go check out the funhouse, but we figured we'd talk to the man who created it first."

Ernest seemed startled by the fact that they knew he was responsible for it. He looked between the two sisters before turning to Samantha, who he must've judged as the one who had more sympathy at that moment. "Are you two cops? I heard they've been looking for me, but I have work to do to get ready for today. I promise I'll go down to the station later. I just wanted to get everything started for the day—"

"We're not cops," Samantha said.

"Parents? Neighbors? I promise, I never had anything to do with that little girl—"

"So, Ernest," Kathy interrupted. "Were you here yesterday? For the preview party those people paid extra for?"

"No, I wasn't. The funhouse was supposed to be closed yesterday."

"And you design the funhouse yourself?" she asked.

He nodded slowly. "Ye-yes, I do."

"And you change the design every stop?"

"I like to keep it fresh," he said. "Just in case someone comes to see us in more than one city. The funhouse is my own special creation."

"So you put together all the surprises inside?" Samantha asked. "By yourself?"

He nodded again. "The only thing I have help with is setting up the tent. After that, the inside is all mine to put together."

"Do you have any help coming up with the surprises?" Kathy asked.

Ernest kept turning his head back and forth between each sister. "No. Everything is my own creation."

"Including the clown inside?" Samantha said.

"There are only pictures of clowns," he said. "The managers wouldn't approve the extra cost of hiring someone specifically for the funhouse, which doesn't have its own charge to enter. It's free. They said they couldn't afford the cost."

"So then how do you explain the clown that attacked that little girl yesterday?" Kathy asked.

"He wasn't—I had no part in that! As far as I know, there are only *pictures* of clowns inside the tent. And who doesn't love clowns?"

"Lots of people, actually," Kathy said.

"If you didn't know he was in there, then who *would* know?" Samantha asked.

Ernest shrugged. "As far as I know, I'm the only one interested in the funhouse tent. Like I said, it's a free attraction. The managers don't put a lot of weight in its value. They only let me do it because I've been with the carnival for nearly forty years and I do most of the work myself."

"It's not like you can really secure the tent, though," Kathy said. "Maybe somebody slipped in, dressed as a clown, and lay in wait for someone to come in."

"Maybe so," he said, gaining a bit more confidence. "But I can't be held responsible for that. If someone snuck into my funhouse, that's not on me. I can only do so much."

Samantha looked over at her sister. He had a point.

"Why should we believe you, Ernest?" Kathy reach over and

plucked a piece of toast from his plate. She was starving.

"Because it's the truth," he said. "Are you sure you're not police officers? If so, I'd like to get a lawyer before I say anything else."

"We're not cops," Samantha said. "But we think we've heard enough. Come on, Kathy. Let's go." She rose, but the younger sister lingered before giving in and following Samantha out of the tent.

"It doesn't make sense," Kathy said after they had exited the tent. "He claims he wasn't at the carnival yesterday, but that just seems awfully convenient. I mean, the attack happened in his funhouse by a clown. And this guy loves clowns!"

Samantha shook her head. "We have to be sure before we do anything rash. Like he said, if someone snuck into the tent and decided to scare the kids, that's not on Ernest."

"I don't think that's likely. Besides, you think Ernest is our guy too, right?"

The older sister shrugged an agreement.

"What did you find out from your professor?"

"Sounds like we're looking at something called a trickster."

Kathy made a face. "A trickster? Never heard of them."

"Loki is probably the most famous."

"But he's locked up."

"Right. So this must be another trickster."

"How confident are you in that assumption?"

Samantha sighed as she looked back to the catering tent. "It seems to make the most sense. Tricksters cause chaos wherever they go—think about all the mishaps that happened yesterday at the party."

"Like you ripping that chair?"

Another sigh. "Yes."

"So it wasn't because you're fat."

"Kathy, can you stay focused? Clearly, I was upset by that." She made a face as a thought occurred to her. "Actually, now that I think about it, I was *very* upset by that. Like, more than I should've been. Do you think the trickster could've been altering my mood with his residual chaotic energy?"

Kathy shrugged. "I guess so."

"Maybe that also explains your brazen attitude today."

"Or maybe it's because I spent the night on the couch sleeping with one ear open listening for the sounds of gagging so I could run in with a bucket before I spent my evening scrubbing vomit from the carpet."

"That was a mouthful." Samantha tucked her hair behind her ears. "Anyway, the point is, we're probably looking at a trickster here."

"Any ideas how to stop him?"

"A stake to the heart dipped in the blood from one of his victims."

Kathy made a face. "Gory."

"Which is why we need to be sure that Ernest is the trickster before we stab the wrong man."

They had made it back to the street. Both sisters had parked near each other. They drove separate, since Kathy came from Jeremy's and Samantha came from home.

"So we should split up," Kathy said.

"That's what I was thinking too. One of us needs to get blood from Kelly to dip the stake in. The other one needs to find more evidence that Ernest is our target. And we need to do it quick. I don't want anyone else getting hurt and I don't think there's any chance that the carnival is going to close the funhouse today."

"Not when it's a main attraction. Even if it is free."

"Right," Samantha said. "Do you think you can keep a cool head if you stay here and look into Ernest more?"

"Why wouldn't I be able to keep a cool head?"

"The trickster creates chaos. You don't know how that will affect you. I think it's safe to say it's already affected both of us. Not at the same time, but it's made us both irritable. His magic is unpredictable. So you have to be careful. We both do."

"I can handle it."

"Get to a phone and call Steven at the house if there's an issue," she said. "I might end up there at some point today. I'm not sure."

"Are you going to get the blood from Kelly, then?"

Samantha let out a deep breath. "I'm going to try. Asking a stranger to let me take a blood sample from his daughter for obscure reasons is not something I wanted to do today, but I think we have the best shot at it with my persuasion power."

"How are your powers doing since your pregnancy?"

The older sister shrugged. "Haven't used them much since that whole thing with Vanita and Oren, so we'll have to see. Still, I think I'll do better than you would without any trickle of persuasion at all."

"I'd like to think I have my own kind of charm," Kathy said.

"None of it magical," Samantha said plainly. "Now let's stop this bastard before he can hurt anymore kids."

CHAPTER 29

Kathy waited until Samantha had driven away before she turned back to the carnival. Now that her sister was gone, she was determined to find Ernest again and make him admit to what he had done to Kelly. With that confession, she'd have no hesitation at all driving a stake through his heart.

As she approached the carnival again, she noticed the crowd had grown. Now, there weren't just crew members, some customers had begun to trickle in as well. The crowd was especially thick around the entrance to the funhouse tent.

Did it really draw that much of a crowd? she wondered. *Was the news about Kelly's attack kept quiet that well? Surely some reporter had picked up the lead.* She hadn't watched the news to know if it had been reported.

The closer she got to the entrance, though, the more she understood the reason for the crowd.

"What's going on?" someone wondered.

"Is everyone okay?"

"How many kids does that make now? Two? Three?"

"Didn't this happen yesterday?"

"What kind of freak show is this?"

Kathy's heart began to race faster as she pushed her way through the crowd. Everyone stopped in a semi-circle outside the funhouse entrance. When Kathy made it to the front, she saw two men carrying out a little boy. He was unconscious, white as a ghost, and looked to be even younger than Kelly.

"What is it about this carnival?" the man beside her wondered.

"This is the second kid who has gone in and had to be carried out," the lady next to him said. "It was a little girl yesterday."

"That's terrible," the man said. "No way in hell I'm going in there. Certainly not sending my kids in."

Balling up her fists, Kathy turned to make her way back out through the crowd. She rounded the funhouse tent, coming around to the back side of it, where she nearly collided with Ernest, who was moving quickly himself. Away from the commotion.

Fleeing.

Kathy pounced, crashing into Ernest and knocking him to

the ground behind the funhouse tent. She pressed her knees into his chest, pinning him into the grass.

"Hey!" he shouted. "Knock it off, lady! Let me go!"

Seizing him by the shoulders, Kathy shook him. "This has to end! Stop hurting these kids!"

If it wasn't for Samantha telling her the only way to stop a trickster, Kathy would've tried to find a way herself right now.

She raised her fist, about to release it to deliver a satisfying blow that would've cracked his nose, but stopped when she saw tears trickling from the old man's face.

"Please!" he whimpered. "Please don't hurt me! I never meant to harm any kids! The funhouse has always been a place where kids go to laugh, not scream!"

Doubt creeped into Kathy's mind. Why would the trickster be crying over his own actions? Then again, Samantha had said he created chaos wherever he went. Maybe this was a ruse.

"I heard the boy screaming and I was coming to rescue him!" he added. "Please! You have to believe me!"

Kathy stiffened her fist, not wanting him to see her letting her guard down. "You're not the one who scared him?"

"No!"

"Where were you yesterday afternoon? When that little girl was attacked?"

"I was visiting my aunt! She lives at 3005 Berkeley Road. Go ask her yourself!"

Sighing, Kathy lowered her arm and slowly pulled herself

away from him. There was no way he pulled that alibi out of thin air. And maybe Samantha was right. Maybe the trickster was nearby and was altering her mood, exaggerating the anger she felt toward Jeremy and projecting it onto this innocent man.

But what if she was wrong and Ernest *was* behind all of this? She didn't want to let him go if he really *was* the trickster.

The crowd was starting to come around the tent, drawn by Ernest's loud pleas. She backed away, giving in to the public pressure she felt. She walked toward her car, shaking her head.

If the trickster could alter her thoughts without even coming into direct contact with her, how was she going to be able to rely on her instincts as a witch?

CHAPTER 30

The trickster stepped into the house thirsty. Tastes. Samples. That's all he had had so far. Barely enough to fully fill him. The party yesterday was supposed to be filled with youthful terrors that should've whet his appetite. Instead, he was starving for more.

"Where have you been all day?" the woman who was supposed to be his wife asked. "You were gone when I woke up and it's—" She glanced up at the clock on the wall above the entertainment center. "—it's been a few hours."

"I went down to the park." He plopped in a chair and stared down at the little girl—Ashley—as she played on the carpet in the center of the living room.

"Why'd you go down there?"

"I don't know. I thought I left a bag of charcoal down there." He had targeted one boy, trying to drain him of all the terror inside him and feast on it. But the boy had fought back, kicked him and shouted before the trickster could really do a lot of damage. When was he going to be able to eat in peace?

He needed another plan. He ached with hunger; felt his energy growing weak.

And yet here sat a little girl, ripe for the taking. But he would need to get her alone. The funhouse tent would be perfect. Word was now spreading that the funhouse was dangerous. It would fuel further worries and fears of the people around it. He would just have to get proactive with the tricks and torments he put people through if they decided to come and investigate. It would take a lot of energy, but if he could fully feed on this little girl, it was energy he could recover.

"Are you going to be in here for a minute?" the woman asked. "I still have to clean up everything from the party yesterday."

He nodded just to shut her up.

She got to her feet and stepped into the kitchen. "It's a shame the party turned out to be a dud. Well, actually, it's a shame what happened to Ned's little girl, Kelly. I tried to call him today, but…"

The trickster tuned out the woman's drawling voice. Instead, he was transfixed on the little girl. She stopped playing and stared at him once she realized her mother had left the room.

They maintained eye contact for a moment before the little girl's bottom lip protruded out and she began crying.

"Is she getting hungry?" the woman called from the kitchen.

The trickster ignored her and continued to stare at the girl. Now was his chance. The girl was scared. She was revved up and he was ready to feast on that fear.

Best of all, they were alone. He could drain her right now and—

"Come here, baby." The woman stepped into the room and scooped up the little girl. "You could've at least picked her up, Charles."

The trickster snapped.

He stood, reached for the little girl, who continued to cry. The woman let him take her, only to realize her mistake when she caught sight of his face. He pushed her to the ground.

The little girl screamed at the top of her lungs, squirming and kicking at the trickster.

"Charles, what are you doing?" the woman asked. "Set her down. Don't hurt her!"

"I'm only doing what I need to do," he replied.

"Put her down!" The woman rose and stepped toward him, reaching for the girl.

The trickster put up his hand, as if to stop her, and created illusions that only she could see. The woman fell backward and slid to the outer wall. She pressed against it, unable to move, her eyes wide with terror.

"How are you doing this?" she asked. "Who are you?"

The trickster soaked in the chaos for a moment. The screaming toddler in his arms, the frightened mother who was helpless to save her daughter. The moment just seemed *perfect* for him.

Offering one last smile to the woman, he stepped to the door.

"Come back here!" the woman called after him, her voice cracking with frenzied emotion. "Put her down! Don't hurt her! Charles! Please! Don't do this!"

The trickster ignored her and stepped outside. Even as he got behind the wheel of the car, he could hear the woman's screams. He drove off with the screaming toddler in his lap and smiled the whole way.

CHAPTER 31

The gas station across the street from Frontier Park had a phone booth around back. Kathy dug out some spare change from her pocket and dialed the house number.

Her heart was still racing from the encounter with Ernest. She almost hurt an innocent man. Could've gotten arrested for assault. She would need to be more careful—and more in check with her emotions—when they finally tracked down the real trickster.

"Hello?" Steven answered on the other end.

"Hey, it's me," Kathy said. "Is Samantha home yet?"

"No, was she supposed to be?"

"I don't know." She ran a hand along her neck under hair and looked out at the parking lot. "She said she was going to

Ned's to ask—to ask for a favor." Steven usually didn't want to hear the details of their jobs as witches. It was a safe bet that he didn't want to hear about his wife asking a traumatized five-year-old for some of her blood.

"Oh," he said. "That's news to me. If she stops here I'll have her get in touch with you. Are you still at Jeremy's?"

"No, I'm calling from a payphone," she said. "I actually need to talk to her soon. Like now, preferably." Sometimes she wished everyone carried phones around with them so she could get in touch with anyone at any time. "Do you know Ned's last name? Maybe you could check the phone book and give me his number."

"I'm sorry, Kathy, I just met him yesterday and I didn't get his last name."

"Yeah, me too." She thought about it, studying the scratches that had been etched into the metal of the booth. "What about Laurel? She should have Ned's number. See if you can find Laurel's number in Sam's address book. I'll call her and get Ned's number."

"Give me a second."

While she waited, Kathy studied the scratches more closely.

"J♥W 1988"

"Mike was here."

"Call Franny for a good time."

She rolled her eyes and didn't want to think about any other activities that might have occurred in this tiny space. At least this booth didn't smell like urine.

"Okay, here it is," Steven said suddenly on the other end. "Are you ready?"

"Ready." Memorization was a skill she had developed through spell writing. She didn't always have a chance to write her spells, so she needed to remember them off hand.

Steven gave her the number, then said, "Do you think Laurel will even be home? I mean, it's a Saturday morning and she seems like the type of person who would be involved in PTA meetings or the neighborhood potluck or something."

"It's worth a shot. I need to get in touch with Samantha and I don't know where Ned lives to go find her. Plus," she added, "I don't want to go too far from the park. Not unless you want to watch it again for a day."

"No way! I put in my time yesterday. I'm looking forward to relaxing today."

Kathy wished her Saturday could be relaxing.

"One of us needs to stay in one piece for when the baby comes," he said. "I'm just glad that my kid won't have to deal with these kind of magical emergencies."

She made a face and pulled the phone away to look at it before pressing it against her ear again. "What are you talking about?"

"The baby," he said. "Samantha said it probably won't have magic because it'll be only half witch."

Why would she lie to him like that? Kathy wondered. *Sure, it'll take years for their baby to first start showing signs of magic, but more likely than not, their child* will *have magic.*

She pushed the issue away for the moment. That was something between husband and wife that they would have to deal with themselves. It was best if Kathy just stayed out of it. "Anyway, thanks for the number."

"No problem. Be careful, Kathy."

When she hung up, she collected the change leftover from her call, fed the coins through the slot again, and dialed the number Steven had rattled off.

The phone rang several times before it stopped. There didn't seem to be anyone on the other end at first.

"Hello?" Kathy said into the phone. "Is anyone there? Hello?"

Silence.

Kathy reached to hang up the phone, but she heard a panicked whisper erupt from the other end.

"I need help!"

"Hello? Laurel? It's me, Kathy. Samantha's sister."

"Kathy, I need you to help me!" Laurel was hysterical. It sounded like she was crying, whispering, struggling through her words.

"What's wrong?"

"It's Charles!"

"Your husband?"

"Whoever that was, it was *not* the man I married! He just

started freaking out! Throwing things, laughing, screaming. He completely lost his mind!"

Charles? Kathy wondered. *That calm man who was grilling yesterday?*

Then Kathy remembered the murmured bickering between him and Laurel. Maybe this was just a marital spat. A fight between husband and wife that had gotten out of hand.

Kathy was getting in the middle of arguments a lot today.

"I was so…I was so…I was so scared!" Laurel wailed. "And then…and then, he…he *took* Ashley! I tried to get her back from him, but he pushed me down! And then he just…he just…he just left!"

"Where did he go?"

"I don't know! You have to help me! You have to get Ashley back! Oh God. I hope he doesn't hurt her!"

"Okay. Okay, just calm down." Kathy tried to think of what to do next. "Um…what were you guys arguing about?"

"That's the thing!" Laurel said. "We weren't even fighting! He just…changed. And then—I don't know. Maybe this didn't happen. Maybe I'm remembering wrong."

"No, what is it? Tell me, Laurel."

"The room was…turning. Changing. I was running to the door, trying to stop Charles from taking her, and then the floor tilted. Like on an incline or something. I swear, it knocked me on my ass and I fell all the way back to the opposite wall. It was—I must be going insane."

Kathy rubbed her forehead, her brain tired from all of the stress. She needed to get in touch with Samantha. Tell her to hurry up. But she had no way of getting in touch with her and Laurel was too shaken up to give her Ned's number or address.

"Okay, you're not going insane," she started. "Just, um, stay put. Stay where you are. If Charles comes back, do you think you can sneak out and go to a neighbor's house? Call 9-1-1 from there? But only if he comes back, okay? I'm going to try to track him down myself."

"Please don't!" she cried. "I don't want anyone to get hurt! I just want my baby back!"

"That's all I'm going to do, Laurel. Trust me. Do you think you can do that?"

"Yes, I can do that," she choked out. "Thank you, Kathy."

Kathy hung up and stepped out of the booth. There was only one place where they knew the trickster was lurking. And it sounded like he had a new victim in mind.

She was going to catch him in the act. Again.

CHAPTER 32

Ned lived in a small brick ranch just outside the city line in Millcreek. This part of the township still mimicked some of the street grid pattern that was prominent in the city, although some streets wound around in a suburban cul-de-sac style. The twisty streets were the reason Samantha had gotten lost when she tried to find his house, taking her longer to get there than she had anticipated.

When she finally knocked on the front door, Ned answered and Samantha offered him a sad smile.

"Samantha," he said. By the drawn out expression on his face, she could tell it had been a long night for him.

"Ned. Hi. I hope you don't mind me dropping by. I just wanted to check on Kelly. How's she doing?"

He rocked his head back and forth. "She's doing okay, considering. Still hasn't gotten that chill out of her. I've given her several warm baths since yesterday, but those apparently didn't do any good. I had to pull out the winter pajamas I had just put away. She's wrapped up in a blanket and heating pad on the couch." He looked back inside, then turned to Samantha. "Why don't you come in? Maybe company will help distract her."

As Samantha followed him through the door, the first thing she noticed was how warm it was. Ned must've turned up the heat to try to help Kelly warm up. "Has she said anything more about what she saw in the tent?"

Ned shook his head as they stepped into the small living room. "Not a thing." Turning to the bundle of blankets and pillows on the couch, he said, "Honey, we have a visitor. Do you remember Samantha? She's one of the people who helped you yesterday."

At first, Samantha didn't even notice that the girl was among the piles of fabric on the couch. It wasn't until the little girl turned her head to look at her father that Samantha noticed the tiny head peeking out of the fort.

Ned took a seat on the footstool in front of her while Samantha stood awkwardly by the door.

"Is it just the two of you?" Samantha asked.

"Kelly's mother and I are divorced," Ned said. "She got into the wrong crowd, so I have full custody."

Samantha nodded. That meant there was likely no one else

in the house. She hated what she was about to do, but at this point, there was no sense in putting it off anymore.

She stepped across the room and knelt down in front of Kelly. "Hello. How are you feeling?"

The little girl shrugged.

"I'm sure not very good," Samantha said. "You know, me and my sister are the ones who stopped that bad man from hurting you in the tent yesterday."

Kelly nodded, clutching at a pillow. "I remember."

"Well, unfortunately, that bad man got away," she said. "We're trying to find him, but—"

"I'm not sure this is appropriate," Ned cut in.

Samantha pushed her persuasion onto him through her words. "Kelly can help us stop the bad man, so we need to have this conversation. Can I continue?"

Ned looked between her and his daughter, contemplating. Obviously, Samantha's magic was slipping. She could thank her pregnancy for that.

Finally, he nodded. "Yeah. Okay. But if she starts getting anxious—"

"It'll be okay." Samantha turned back to Kelly. "Do you think you could help us stop the bad man?"

The little girl clutched the pillow tighter. "I'm scared."

"Oh, honey, I know. But the best part is, you don't ever have to see him again."

"Then how can I help?"

"Well…" Here came the moment of truth. She tried her best to radiate her persuasion to both Ned and Kelly. It was an act she would've had no problem doing pre-pregnancy, but the growing fetus in her belly was throwing off everything she thought she knew about herself. "My sister and I found a way to stop him. To kill him."

Ned sucked in a quick breath of air behind her, surprised she had said that, but he offered no objections.

"How?" the little girl asked in the smallest voice.

"Do you know how they stop vampires?"

"Vampires?" She shook her head.

"A wooden stake right through the heart." Samantha pointed to the spot on her chest to further paint the picture.

"Um…Samantha…" Ned started behind her, but she focused on persuading them both and continued.

"The bad man who hurt you is kind of like a vampire," she said. "The only way to stop him from hurting other kids is to drive a wooden stake through his heart. But there's more to it than that."

Now she had the girl's attention. "Like what?"

"Well, this is where you come in," Samantha said. "You can help turn something bad that happened to you into a good thing."

"How?"

"The bad man is vulnerable when the kids he tried to scare get brave with him," Samantha said. "Do you know what 'vulnerable' means?"

"Weak?"

"Right! Do you think you can be brave for me?"

"Maybe."

"What are you asking her to do?" Ned asked.

Samantha took in a deep breath. The maternal instinct she was developing told her that this was wrong. But she also knew that this was the only way to stop the trickster.

"I need…some of your blood," Samantha said to the girl, using extent of her power. The exertion made her tired, but she pressed on. "It's the only way to stop him."

"And how do you know this?" Ned asked.

"You just need to trust me."

"Sam, I don't know if this…" He trailed off and looked between the two of them. Clearly, he was torn between his objections and Samantha's magic.

"I just need a little." Samantha reached in her purse and produced a syringe that she had picked up at the drug store on her way over. "You can do it yourself if you'd like. I just need enough to dip the end of the stake in. Please, you guys. This will stop him from hurting anymore kids. And Kelly, it may actually help you feel better afterward."

She had a running theory that the trickster's effects lasted as long as the trickster did. It was the same way with witches. If a witch casted a spell on someone and then they died the next day, the spell was usually broken because the witch who cast it was no longer alive.

At least, she hoped that was the case with the trickster.

Ned considered the request further, then looked to Kelly. "What do you think, peanut?"

"I want to stop the bad man."

Samantha smiled. "Way to be brave, Kelly. I'm proud of you."

Ned hesitated, then reached for the syringe.

As Samantha watched him extract the blood from his daughter, she felt the gnawing at the pit of her stomach that told her she was a horrible person for asking this of them.

But it was the only way.

CHAPTER 33

After the second child had been pulled out of the funhouse tent earlier that morning, it had been closed to the public while the police investigated it. As Kathy approached it, she saw one uniformed officer standing guard at the police line. The yellow police tape blocked the front entrance. Closer to the entrance, two detectives in gray suits stood together, talking quietly with each other.

There was only one way Kathy was going to get inside unnoticed and she needed to be quick about it.

Walking up, she proceeded with confidence and purpose. As if she belonged to the cadre of police lingering outside the tent. In a swift motion, she froze the two detectives with one hand, then quickly raised the other to freeze the uniformed officer.

TRICKSTER

Slipping under the tape, she hurried to the canvas flap leading into the funhouse tent. Before she completely disappeared inside, she waved her hand behind her. In an instant, all three unfroze, completely unaware that time had stopped for only a moment.

Kathy wasn't sure if there would be more detectives or officers or crime scene investigators inside, so she was prepared to freeze again in case she came across anyone.

Or anything, she realized afterward.

If the trickster could alter reality, maybe he could take the shape of a police officer and then morph into something more sinister that would scare even Kathy. Maybe the trickster only chose a clown to scare the children.

She chose the pathway she and Samantha had taken the day before, following the darkening hallway through the maze that zigzagged through the tent.

"Charles!" she called out. "I know you're the trickster! Show yourself!"

There was no response.

The noise from the carnival outside seemed to die off, as if she had entered a whole separate world. Worse, the light faded faster than it seemed to the first time she and Samantha had entered the tent.

"Ashley! Your mom sent me! You're going to be okay, sweetie!"

Still nothing.

Heart racing, Kathy continued on.

Up at the next bend, she saw lights coming from around the corner and she figured it was the room with the strobe lights they had stumbled through yesterday. With a newfound resolve, she pressed on, stopping short when she saw a shadow move across the light.

Is that a police officer? she wondered. *Ashley? The trickster?*

"Hello?" she called out in a weak voice. "Is someone there?"

She regretted coming in alone. This place was giving her the creeps.

Sucking in a deep breath, she tried to get a handle on her nerves before moving on.

The trickster feeds on fear, she reminded herself.

Gaining the courage to move on, she came around the corner and entered the room around the corner to find—

No one.

She looked around, debating whether the trickster had already begun to play mind tricks on her. Making her see things that weren't there. But even though she was nervous, she wasn't terrified. She'd been in scarier situations before. Maybe that was part of his plan. To amp up the fear little-by-little, making her think she was safe until it was too late to back out.

But Kathy was a witch. She had a duty to save Ashley and stop the trickster. Or at least prevent him from hurting anyone else until Samantha could get here with the stake.

She left the empty room and moved on. The next hallway

started out perfectly normal…and then the muddied ground below her began to become softer, sucking in her feet with every step. Each footfall resulting in a loud *slop* when she went to lift her foot out of the loose mud.

This is just a trick, she told herself. *Keep going. It'll stop.*

But the mud only deepened. To the point where Kathy was knee-deep in it, then waist deep. She paused to rest, feeling herself sinking lower. If she didn't keep moving, she'd be stuck permanently.

Using all of her strength, she forced one leg in front of the other, fighting the resistance pushing back at her. Slowly, she began to feel the ground firm up beneath her.

On the other side of the mud pit, she paused and leaned forward onto her muddied knees to catch her breath. Her legs were sore and tired from the effort, but she knew she needed to continue.

The next corner brought a new surprise. It was nothing that she noticed at first. Again, it wasn't until she moved further down the corridor that she noticed the room was getting larger. Or rather, that *she* was shrinking.

With each step forward, she found herself closer to the ground, even with her legs fully extended beneath her. Eventually, she was hiking between blades of grass. An ant crawled in front of her, larger than her own body, and she stifled a scream.

If she screamed, the trickster would come to feed off of her fear. And if she was this small, there was no way her magic would have any effect on him.

Okay, she said with another deep breath. *Stay calm. Don't panic. Last time, the trick disappeared the more I walked on. Let's just keep going.*

She took a step forward and the ant turned on her. It's pincers clanged together and it held its ground.

Kathy stepped to the side to take cover behind a blade of grass, but the ant moved on her quickly. Throwing up her hands, she reflexively used her power.

A moment passed. She opened her eyes and saw the ant had frozen, mid-step.

Sucking in a deep breath, she carefully stepped around the towering bug and broke out into a run, hoping not to encounter anything else.

The more she ran, the larger she became. Soon, she was back to her normal size and nearly collided with the wall of the tent. Cutting to the left at the last minute, she found herself face-to-face with the clown.

The trickster.

He sneered at her, then turned and fled in the opposite direction.

He wants me to chase him, she thought. It was probably a trap, but she wanted to catch him. To find out where he was keeping Ashley.

"Get back here!" she called after him. "Tell me where Ashley is!"

TRICKSTER

Breaking into a run, she chased after the clown. She made it around the next corner and stopped dead when she found herself surrounded by something completely unexpected.

She stood in the entryway of a loft apartment. The space was large. There were enormous windows in the wall opposite her, while the outer walls were brick. There was an open kitchen to one end with a hallway beyond that leading to additional rooms. Against the inner wall was a metal staircase that led to a loft area with another room above.

"What the hell?" Kathy stepped in further and looked around. Everything was so vivid. So real. She reached down and touched a fluffy pillow on the couch.

This can't be the trickster's illusion, she thought. *It's not his style. He's been doing* Alice in Wonderland *stuff. Not this.*

Her thoughts were cut off when the door she had just stepped through opened and Jeremy entered.

"Hey babe." He set his briefcase down on the table beside the door, then walked up and kissed her on the lips. "How was your day?"

She stared at him, startled by the way the light reflected off the gold band on his ring finger.

"Are you okay?" he asked.

Kathy looked down at her own hand and saw a diamond ring sitting on her own ring finger.

CHAPTER 34

Honey!" Samantha called when she walked through the front door. "Do you know if we have any stakes in the garage? They need to be wooden."

Steven was spread out on the couch with the TV remote in his hand. He sat up and took a deep breath, looking around. Clearly, he had been napping on the couch.

"Glad to see you're enjoying your day off," she said with a smirk.

"I think I deserve it after sitting around the park all afternoon yesterday." He rubbed his eyes. "Why do you need a stake?"

"To kill the trickster," she said. "Remember, that's what we figured out yesterday in the library? Do you think we have any?

I know my dad used to, but honestly, I haven't really been in the garage much since he disappeared. You spend more time in there."

Steven was by no means "handy," but he'd been doing most of the yard work and outside maintenance of the sisters' house long before he ever moved in. When Samantha's dad disappeared, she had been so focused on paying the taxes and the insurance to keep the house that she had let some of the outside work go. The first time Steven came over, he saw the leaves piled in the corner by the front stoop, the overgrown lawn, and the withering flower pots and told her he'd take care of it. He'd basically been doing it ever since.

"Wait a minute," he said. "Did Kathy ever get in touch with you?"

"No, why?"

"She called here about half an hour ago looking for you. Said she needed to talk to you right away."

Samantha shot to her feet. "Why didn't you call me?"

"She said you were at that guy Ned's house and I didn't know his number."

"Did she say what it was about?"

"No. But she did ask for Laurel's number and I gave her that."

Samantha tucked her hair behind her ears. Kathy must have found something or heard something that required her to go after the trickster alone.

How could I let us split up? Samantha berated herself.

She couldn't help but think about last Halloween, when they had split up. It had nearly cost her her life—and Steven's, along with the other hostages the shapeshifter had taken. Was that the same situation Kathy was in now?

Luckily, Samantha knew where Kathy probably was: the funhouse tent at the park.

"You think something bad happened to Kathy," Steven said, reading his wife's expression. It wasn't a question.

She took in a deep breath. "I'm not sure. But here's what we're going to do. You go out into the garage and get me a wooden stake, please. Preferably something with a point. I need to drive that thing through the sucker's heart."

"And that'll kill him?"

"Hopefully. I'll see if I can find any potions that I already have made that could help us. I doubt it, but it can't hurt to look."

"You look scared," he said.

"Nervous. Do you think Kathy would go looking for the trickster without me?"

"Well, when it comes to doing the right thing, the two of you are pretty much the same," he said. "So the better question is, if the roles were reversed, would you?"

She thought about it, then nodded. "In a heartbeat."

"Then there's your answer."

Samantha started toward the backdoor. "We need to get the

stake and get down to the park."

"You're not going alone. Not when you're like this."

"You're not coming in with me," she said.

"Then at least let me drive you."

She looked back at him and was reminded of why she loved her husband. He was dedicated to her, no matter what.

"Let's hurry," she said. "We don't know how long Kathy's got before the trickster gets to her."

CHAPTER 35

"Did you pick up Ruby yet?" Jeremy moved to the kitchen and pulled out a bottle of beer.

"Ruby?"

He hooked an eyebrow as he twisted off the cap. "Our daughter?"

Kathy's stomach dropped. *Daughter? Since when did that happen?*

"You were supposed to pick her up from my parents' on your way home from work," he explained.

She had no idea where "work" was for her, but as far as she knew Jeremy's parents lived between the lake and the airport, so she must've worked out that way if it was expected that she'd pick up their daughter.

It was still too mind-boggling to wrap her head around the fact that she had a daughter.

Jeremy took a sip of his beer, then set it on the kitchen island. "I guess I can call my mom and see if she'd drop her off." He glanced at his watch. "Maybe I can catch her before rush hour really sets in. Speaking of, Jameson should be getting off the bus anytime now."

"Jameson is…our son?" So she apparently had two kids that she didn't remember having? And a husband she didn't remember marrying? At least she knew who Jeremy was. He was the only familiar thing about this whole place.

"Yes! The bus driver won't let him off if one of us isn't down on the street to get him. Otherwise, we'll have to go down to the school and pick him up and get another lecture from the principal about being a responsible parent and child safety and all of that bullshit."

Kathy nodded slowly, still processing. She moved toward the door.

So she was a wife and a mother. Apparently not a very good mother, if she couldn't even remember her own children or the responsibilities that came with them. At least their apartment seemed nice, although she had a suspicion that that was due to the money Jeremy brought in and not her.

Kids? she wondered. *Marriage?*

Why didn't she remember experiencing any of it? Did she have a large wedding, or something small like Samantha's? Did she and Jeremy go on a honeymoon? Where? How did he propose? Was she sure the answer was 'yes' when he had asked?

And the kids. Were they planned? Were they a surprise? Were they a joy to have or a reminder that she was trapped in a marriage and a normal life? Did she enjoy having a normal life, or did she yearn for something different? Did her children think she was a good mother?

"When you get back, you can start dinner," Jeremy told her as he took a seat on the couch.

She nodded, not wanting to say another word that would draw up more suspicion.

When did I learn how to cook a full meal?

"Oh, and I'm out of clean socks," he added. "So if you could run down to the laundromat after we eat, I'd appreciate it."

Kathy opened the apartment door and stole one last look at her supposed husband. He downed a big swig of his beer, extended his legs up on the glass coffee table, and reached for the phone on the end table.

Helping around the house was apparently not even on his radar.

And this is the man I married? she said to herself.

That thought alone was enough to send chills up and down her spine.

CHAPTER 36

There was a crowd of people visiting the carnival when Samantha and Steven arrived. Reaching up on her tiptoes, Samantha tried to look over everyone's heads to see if the funhouse tent was open. Meanwhile, she kept a firm grip on Steven's hand as she pushed through the crowd toward their destination.

When they reached the funhouse, Samantha was startled to see police tape barricading the entrance and a uniformed officer standing guard. It was a stark contrast from the whimsical music playing from somewhere down the midway.

"What's going on?" she asked out loud, but her words were lost in the commotion of the carnival.

"Are you sure Kathy's inside?" Steven asked.

She nodded. "She would've found us by now if she wasn't."

"Are you sure she would in this crowd? There's a lot of people here."

"Yes, she would've found a way." Samantha searched for any other entrance to the tent. She considered going around the side and pulling up the canvas wall to sneak underneath, but she had a feeling that whatever magic was on this tent was only activated by going through the front entrance.

Besides, she knew the way to the center of the tent from the front entrance. That's where she wanted to go because it was where she had seen the trickster before. If she entered from the side, she had no way of knowing if she was on the right path.

Samantha walked up to the police line and called to the uniformed officer. "Excuse me!" She waved to get his attention.

He waved back, but didn't move.

"Why is this blocked off?" she called to him.

He made an exaggerated show of setting aside his entry log book and walking up to her. "What?"

"How come this is blocked off?" she repeated. "I was looking forward to seeing it. I heard great things about it."

"There's an ongoing investigation," he said. "That's all I can tell you."

"What are you investigating?" She laced these words with her persuasion. It worked for Ned and Kelly, so she was confident she could get it to work on the officer, even despite her pregnancy.

"Two little kids were scared shitless in there," he said without hesitation. "To the point where the boy is being hospitalized. The boy's mother called, claiming the carnival is responsible for child endangerment, so we were called in."

"The boy? I only heard about the girl yesterday. When was the other attack?"

"I can't say whether or not it was an *attack*," he said. "That's what we're looking into. But it was earlier today. Right when they first opened."

Samantha shook her head. Now she was definitely convinced that her sister was in there. Hopefully it wasn't too late.

"Do the police have any idea who is behind all this?" Steven asked behind her.

"I can't say anything about the open investigation," he said.

Samantha brushed it aside. The officer wasn't an open book with Steven because he wasn't under the influence of magic with Steven's questions.

It didn't matter anyway. She didn't need to know who. She was more concerned with finding Kathy because her sister had likely already figured it all out on her own.

"Any chance you can let me in there?" she asked.

"Sam," Steven said as a warning.

She shot him a look, telling him to drop it without a single word exchanged between them. Turning back to the officer, she flashed a smile—and her power.

"We have the crime scene unit in there checking for forensics," he said.

"I won't bother them," she said. "I promise."

The officer nodded. "All right. But if anyone asks, I'll deny letting you in."

"Perfect."

He lifted up the police tape for her to enter. As she ducked behind the tent flap, she looked back and tried to offer Steven a reassuring look.

The worry on his face made it apparent that she hadn't comforted him in any way.

CHAPTER 37

The funhouse tent was quiet and not that difficult to navigate. So far, it was too easy for Samantha's taste, putting her on high alert as she moved through the labyrinth. The total silence was eerie. The lack of tricks and surprises was troubling.

Did the trickster already move out? Was he just preoccupied now that he had Kathy to torment? Or was he trying to pull Samantha into a trap?

Even if that last one was true, she knew she'd continue regardless. Kathy was somewhere in this tent and Samantha intended to find her.

Finally, Samantha came around a corner and was face-to-face with her sister. Kathy was suspended in the air, her head rolled back and her arms slack at her sides.

Samantha reached out to wake her sister up, but the clown materialized in front of her with a plume of black smoke. She recoiled and took a step backward.

"Thought you'd be able to just walk right in here, did you?" he snarled with an exaggerated smile, accentuated by the makeup smeared on his face.

Before Samantha had a chance to react, the clown held out his hand, pursed his lips, and blew powder from the palm of his hand into her face. She coughed and swatted at the air.

When she opened her eyes, the clown still stood in front of her. Behind him, Kathy was still suspended in the air.

"Shoot," the clown murmured. "Messed that one up." He turned and ran away, past Kathy.

Pulling the wooden stake out of her bag, Samantha charged after him. On the car ride over, she had dipped the tip in Kelly's blood and watched as it soaked into the wood.

The clown laughed maniacally as Samantha chased him, rounding corners, dodging swinging pendulums or faces that popped out to scare visitors. Samantha had the advantage. The clown was the first to encounter these obstacles and she had a split second to watch how he dodged them to follow in the same path. And that advantage was enough to help her to gain some ground.

Whipping around another corner, Samantha lunged, wrapping her arms around the clown's middle and knocking him to the ground in the center room where they had stopped him from hurting Kelly the day before.

The clown kicked and pushed at the ground to get away from her, but Samantha held firm and put all of her weight on him to keep him in place.

He raised his arms, trying to push her off of him. She moved her knees up and pinned his elbows down to the ground. Behind her, his knees kicked up and hit her in the back, but she ignored the impacts.

Raising the stake above her head, she brought it down hard into the clown's chest, driving it straight into his heart. He convulsed, then went limp.

Samantha sat back, her own chest heaving. She watched curiously as the clown's face began to morph into Steven's.

She shot to her feet and looked down with dismay. Blood seeped onto the ground beneath him, spilled out of his mouth. His eyes were still wide open with shock. But he was unmistakably her husband.

"No," she muttered to herself. "No, you were the trickster! He was *right here*! I *saw* him! This is—this can't be—*no!*"

A sob erupted out of her. She dropped to her knees again and cradled her husband's limp body, holding it closer to herself as she cried.

CHAPTER 38

Is that about done yet?" Jeremy called from his place on the couch. He had another beer in his hand. The kids sat on the couch beside him arguing over a toy.

Meanwhile, Kathy was in the kitchen trying not to burn anything. She had chicken in the oven, pasta on the stove, and she was prepping a salad on the counter. She had also been informed by Jameson that he didn't want peanut butter and jelly in his lunch tomorrow, he wanted something else, to which Jeremy had piped up and told her that she could just pack the leftovers in his lunch tomorrow to make it easier for her.

Add making everyone's lunches to her to-do list.

"It's probably going to be a bit." She grabbed a spoon and stirred the noodles, checking the remaining time on the timer for the chicken as she did. Still another three minutes. "Unless you want to help."

"I'm tired," he said. "I've been working all day. That's why I'm hungry. Sheesh, at this rate I would've been better off getting something on my way home."

"I'm working as fast as I can by myself," she said.

Figuring the pasta was done, she dumped them in a strainer in the sink, then returned to the cutting board where she chopped up the rest of the tomatoes. She had already shredded lettuce and added cucumbers.

The oven dinged and Kathy left the salad to pull out the chicken. A puff of smoke came out of the oven door and she immediately began to cough and wave it out of her face.

"What the hell?" Jeremy shot to his feet and ran beside her.

"Mom's burning the house down!" the kids yelled.

Jeremy slammed the oven door shut as Kathy dropped the oven pan on the stove, still coughing. "This whole place is going to smell all night now!"

"It's not like I did it—" She broke off for a coughing fit. "—like I did it on purpose!"

"You have to keep an eye on these things!" he bellowed. "Now what are we going to eat?"

She smoothed out the hairs on the top of her head. Her hair had long ago been put up into a bun, away from her face. "I don't know, Jeremy."

"You think we can afford pizza every night? For God's sake,

you're a mother. I thought you knew how to cook?"

"Well, if I had a little help in here, maybe this wouldn't have happened. You could've gotten up off your ass and asked if I needed anything!" She looked over at the two kids. They were hers, yet quite honestly they were also perfect strangers. Either way, she didn't think they should be witnessing this marital spat.

Pulling off her apron, she tossed it on the counter then walked down the hall to the bedroom she supposedly shared with Jeremy.

"Where are you going?" He followed her.

"I need a break," she said.

"A break? What, are you going to leave?"

"For a little while, yeah," she said. "Just to clear my head." She stepped into their en suite bathroom and splashed water in her face.

"And where are you going to go?"

Reaching for a towel, she said, "I don't know. Maybe to see my sister."

"Samantha? You're talking to her again?"

She cocked an eyebrow. "Wasn't aware I ever stopped."

"It's been *years*," he said. "About as long as we've been married."

Kathy shook her head and stepped back into the bedroom. "That doesn't make sense. My sister and I are inseparable."

"What happened to you?" he asked. "How can you not remember this? Ever since you renounced your responsibilities as a witch, you two have gone your separate ways."

She froze in her tracks and stared at him. First, hearing Jeremy talk about her being a witch was a shock. Then, there was that other piece of information he had enlightened her on. "Renounced my responsibilities as a witch?"

He nodded. "You did some voodoo stuff too. Made it so you didn't even have magic anymore so you wouldn't be tempted."

That was too far of a stretch. Too far out of the realm of reality. This whole situation seemed to be bending reality as it was. Kathy knew she would never stop being a witch, especially if that meant cutting her sister out of her life.

This wasn't right. Not just the fact that she apparently wasn't a witch anymore, but this apartment, the kids, her marriage to Jeremy, all of it. It wasn't her life. None of it was real. It was a fabrication. An illusion.

Reality came rushing back to Kathy in an instant. This was all the work of the trickster. None of this was real, no matter how real it felt. She was stuck in a trance, orchestrated by a being known for illusions.

Before her eyes, Jeremy disappeared in a swirl, followed by the apartment. For a moment, all she saw was darkness. Then suddenly, she fell hard on the ground inside the funhouse tent.

She was finally back to reality.

CHAPTER 39

Looking over from where she lay on the ground, Kathy saw Samantha hovering in the air, head rolled back and arms slack. On the ground beneath her lay the wooden stake dipped in blood.

"Sam." Kathy reached for her sister. As soon as their hands touched, the older witch fell to the ground and her eyes fluttered open. Her breath quickened to the point of hyperventilating and tears spilled from her eyes.

"Sam!" Kathy called. "Samantha, relax!"

"Steven! Where's Steven? He's—I—"

Kathy pulled her sister close for a hug. It was her effort to console her big sister, but if Kathy were being honest, the hug helped calm her down as well. "Shh," she muttered in

Samantha's ear, "Steven's not here. It was just an illusion. I had one too."

Samantha pulled away. "An illusion? The trickster?"

Kathy nodded. "I didn't see him touch me or cast a spell or anything, but he must have."

"He can alter reality. Make us see whatever he wants us to see. I saw—Steven…" She sucked in a deep breath. "I was chasing the trickster. I caught up to him, pinned him down, and stabbed him with this." She held up the wooden stake that lay on the ground beside her. "But then he turned into Steven and—and—" Her breath caught and she brought a hand to her mouth as more tears spilled out. "I killed him!"

Kathy pulled her sister in for another hug. "Shh, no you didn't. It wasn't real."

"It felt real enough."

"But Steven's alive and well. Unfortunately, so is the trickster."

Samantha shook her head. "Even if we get the bastard, he still put that memory in my head. I can't unsee it."

"I know. But you'll have to replace that memory with happy ones. And with the baby coming, that'll be easy to do."

Samantha nodded. "What did you see?"

"A day in the life as Jeremy's wife."

Samantha furrowed her brow.

"The illusion was that I was Jeremy's wife," she explained. "We had two kids, lived in an apartment, I apparently worked—

both out of the home and around the apartment. I was completely domesticated, like a so-called *respectable* woman. But I was miserable, Sam. Jeremy was lazy. I was overwhelmed. What broke me out of it was that Jeremy said that you and I didn't talk anymore. And that I had stopped being a witch. Apparently removed my powers and everything."

"You wouldn't ever do that."

"Exactly." Kathy grinned. "And now I'm sure that I don't want any of the rest of it to come true."

Samantha frowned. "It was an illusion created by the trickster. You can't be certain that that's the kind of marriage you and Jeremy would have."

Kathy averted her eyes and sighed. "That's the thing, though. I can already see the signs between me and Jeremy leading to the type of relationship I saw in the illusion. And that's not what I want. If I decide to get married, it's going to be a partnership. If I have kids, I don't want to feel like I'm a slave to them. I want to continue to have my own life. And that means I need someone who will be supportive of that." She shook her head. "I'm not sure I see that in Jeremy."

They were quiet for a moment and then Samantha finally asked, "Was he drinking in the illusion?"

"He wasn't drunk, but he was drinking." She sucked in a shuddering breath. "Anyway, we don't have time to chitchat anymore. We need to stop the trickster—Charles."

"Charles?" Samantha rose to her feet. "It's not Ernest?"

Kathy shook her head and wiped the grass from her legs. "Nope. He wasn't even in the tent when a second kid was attacked." She led them through the maze as she talked. "And I called Laurel. She was freaking out because Charles started acting crazy. She said the room was turning, so I figured that's a surefire sign that Charles is the guy and he was spinning tricks on her. But he has Ashley."

"Oh no!"

"We need to find her."

They made two more turns and then stumbled into the center of the maze, coming to the clearing where they had seen the trickster with Kelly. It was a similar scene when they entered, only this time the clown was feasting on Ashley's terrorized screams.

"Hey!" Samantha shouted. "Let her go!"

The trickster turned. Kathy extended her arms outward to freeze the trickster and Ashley.

Except Kathy's magic only worked on Ashley. Immediately her cries stopped as she was frozen in time. The clown, however, continued to step toward them, his sinister smile growing wider the closer he got.

"Here's a fun fact for you girls." His voice had a slight lisp and a heavy wet sound with each word. "I am immune to witchcraft."

CHAPTER 40

So, what?" Samantha asked. "Are you acting like a shapeshifter now? Kidnapping people to steal their identity?"

The clown clutched his belly as his head rolled back in laughter. "Ahaha! I am so much *more* than a mere *shapeshifter*! I can distort time and reality. I can make anything happen. You want to see pigs fly? All it would take is the snap of my fingers. Nuclear holocaust? Polar ice caps melting? Or perhaps you're more creative than that. What if the earth were flat? Or the sun exploded? What if you'd never been born? What if magic didn't exist?"

The sisters both stared at him as he rambled. Samantha judged the distance between them and Ashley. She wondered if she'd be able to grab her and escape through the opening on the other side of the room. Of course, that would leave Kathy essentially defenseless if her magic didn't work on him.

"You see," he continued, "I exist outside the realm of reality. I'm immortal. I've been around for centuries. Existed long before witches. Although, I will say, I think it's cute that you try to protect these humans. Meanwhile, I see them as simply walking meals. A tasty little bunch, you all are. Like livestock awaiting slaughter." He brought a hand to his mouth and snickered. "I know you're not supposed to play with your food, but I just can't help it. You're all so *entertaining*!" He erupted into more demented giggles.

"So did Charles ever exist?" Kathy asked. "Or have you been him all along, playing along just so you could get into a friendly neighborhood filled with kids? That's *perverted*, by the way. Absolutely disgusting."

"Very inquisitive, you are," he said. "But to answer your question, no, I would never *lay* with my food. That would be like you marrying the cow that'll eventually be butchered for the burger you'll enjoy the next day." He shook his head. "It's just not right. Even for my warped mentality."

"At least we can agree that you're crazy," she muttered.

"I arrived into town and stumbled on poor Charles. It was just too good of an opportunity to pass up," he said. "I learned he had a child—a young one, at that. One that I could scare without much effort. Once I laid eyes on her I could tell she was a screamer."

Samantha balled up her fists. She hated the way he was

talking about sweet little Ashley, who was frozen behind him with terror on her face. She was innocent. She didn't deserve this kind of torment.

Worse, Samantha wondered if her own unborn child would be subjected to this kind of ridicule.

"As I got closer," the trickster continued, "I heard her mother talking about a birthday party with other children and, well, there was an even greater opportunity I couldn't pass up."

Samantha noticed that Kathy had been inching around the perimeter of the tent. She was almost out of the trickster's peripheral vision and ready to make a grab for Ashley and run.

Be careful. Samantha pushed the message into Kathy's head.

Keep him talking, Kathy replied in her own head.

"But you only targeted one girl at the party," Samantha said. "Why not wait until today to target a larger group when the carnival opened?"

"Ah, you see, just like humans, I get greedy. I couldn't help myself when that little girl ventured in here unaccompanied."

"So you're not perfect."

He laughed. "Who said I was perfect? I'm also not stupid."

In the blink of an eye, a second clown appeared right in front of Kathy. He was an exact copy of the one talking to Samantha.

"You were going to try to make a run for it with the girl," the second one told Kathy. "That's not a smart move. As long as you're within this tent, I can do whatever I want with you.

Actually, I can do whatever I want beyond this tent, but there are many more variables to maintain outside of a controlled environment such as this."

"I told you," the first one said to Samantha. "I can manipulate reality, which means I can create as many copies of myself as I want."

A third clown appeared, then a fourth, followed by a fifth and a sixth. One-by-one, the trickster multiplied, duplicating his form until he took up all the available space in the room.

Samantha looked around and drew her shoulders in, trying to stay as far away from the trickster clones as possible. "Kathy!"

From somewhere in the trickster crowd, she called back, "I'm okay! For now."

"I can also do anything I want to," he said. "Alter the laws of physics for a moment?" In unison, the tricksters each lifted one hand each.

Samantha felt a magical energy pull her up into the air. Over the heads of the tricksters, she saw Kathy was suspended the same way.

"Then put them back!" The trickster cackled as the group each flicked their hands in the same direction, sending the girls flying back into the opening they had come from.

Together, they crashed on the ground, then immediately shot to their feet. Samantha pressed a hand protectively against her belly and hoped all this falling wasn't hurting the baby.

"We have to get to Ashley!" Kathy charged at the tricksters

blocking the entry into the room, but there were too many of them. She collided into them and then bounced off. They were creating a human shield.

From inside the room, they could hear Ashley's cries resume. Kathy's magic had worn off.

CHAPTER 41

What's the matter, witch?" the trickster called from the voices of every duplicate. "Can't quite get through?" He broke into maniacal laughter.

Kathy turned to her sister. "Okay, we need a plan. How are we going to get him to just one so we can drive the stake through his heart?" She looked around. "Where is the stake?"

"Back in the room," Samantha said. "I dropped it before he threw us aside like yesterday's trash."

"Damn. And if we run back through the maze, who's to say he won't put us through more tricks and illusions? Maybe we won't even be able to break out of them this time."

"But if we manage to get him down to one, we can get back inside, grab the stake, and finish the job."

"Oh sure. No problem," Kathy said sarcastically. "How are we going to do that if he's immune to witchcraft? It's not like I can come up with a spell."

"We're going to have to find a way to convince him," Samantha said. "And I can't use my persuasion, either. Or peek through his head telepathically. So we're going to have to rely on our own charms."

"So what are we going to do?"

Samantha took a deep breath. "Do you think he'll listen to us?"

"Do you have something in mind?"

"Maybe."

Kathy stood aside as her sister approached the clones blocking their entry into the center room.

"Come up with a *plan*, have you?" the trickster asked. He cackled, his face turning up into his frightening smile.

"You've trapped us," Samantha said. "There's nowhere we can go now. Not without Ashley, anyway."

"That appears to be the case, yes," he replied. "And if you run, I'll have time to lock the two of you in an illusion, feast on the girl, then the two of you. This little girl makes three children that I've fed on, plus if I add in the two of you—witches, no less. I should regain the strength I lost and be able to move on to the next town to torment."

"Before you go, though, can I ask a favor?" Samantha asked.

The trickster cackled. "How rich! Yes, I suppose I could

humor you for a bit. What is it you desire?"

"You can alter reality all you want?" the older witch asked. "No limits?"

"I thought you wanted a favor, not an interrogation?"

"Just answer the question."

"There are a certain level of…*limitations* I have, yes. But I'd be a fool to reveal them to you. I may be a bit crazy, but I'm not stupid."

"Oh, of course not," Kathy murmured.

"Can you turn into my husband?" Samantha asked, ignoring Kathy. "That illusion you put me in before…I saw some things that I don't want to come true. And if you're going to kill us now, I want to be able to tell Steven—whether he's actually here or not—that I'm sorry for what he married."

The clown hooked an eyebrow. "Is that it?"

"I don't want an illusion," she said. "I want to see his face. I need to see his face."

"And for you?" he asked. The many heads turned to Kathy, which she found unsettling and made goosebumps prickle all over her skin.

She held up her hands. "I'm good."

The heads turned back to Samantha. "So just the husband, then?"

She nodded. "Please."

"Oh, I get a 'please' with it," he cheered. "Well, how about that?"

Samantha looked somber. "The sooner the better. I just want to get this over with."

In an instant, the many tricksters converged back into one. The sight was disorienting, making Kathy take a couple steps backwards. When the trickster was back in one form, he started to morph into an identical copy of Steven. Again, it was eerie to see him knowing that it wasn't actually him. Kathy had flashbacks to last Halloween when they faced the shapeshifter.

"I'm here, darling," he said with a half-grin. "What is it you want—"

"Don't talk," Samantha said. "Just…stand there."

The trickster Steven lost his trying-too-hard suave demeanor and just stood and looked at her.

"Steven, I'm sorry," she said. "I'm sorry that I'm not the wife you deserve. That our child is going to probably have the same traits as me—hopefully they mostly get yours. You deserve the world and I feel like I keep falling short in showing my appreciation for you. Steven, you're—"

The trickster Steven's eyes grew large. Both sisters watched curiously as blood sputtered out of his mouth and down his chest where…the point of the blood-dipped stake poked through.

Samantha let out a yelp and jumped back as the trickster fell forward onto the ground. Behind him, stood Steven—the real Steven. His chest heaved and his hands shook, but it was him.

CHAPTER 42

Samantha rushed up and wrapped her arms around her husband. Her real husband. She squeezed him tight and refused to let him go, finding comfort in his arms tightening around her.

Over his shoulder, she watched as Kathy rushed to Ashley, who lay screaming on the ground. Scooping her up in her arms, Kathy cooed and shushed the little girl, even though she continued to cry.

Finally, Steven pulled away from Samantha. "That was the plan, right?"

She shook her head. "I was stalling. I thought maybe if I could get him to talk then Kathy could sneak around and get Ashley, but..." She looked up at him and offered a tearful smile. "You did great."

He shook out his hands. "That's some kind of thrill, isn't it? I'm a little shaken up from it."

She nodded. "Killing evil beings isn't fun, but it's necessary." She pointed to Kathy and Ashley. The little girl had finally stopped crying, though her breath still caught in her throat and her chest still heaved. "Saving people like her makes it all worth it."

They walked out of the funhouse without any issues. The tricks that Ernest had installed were nothing compared to the trickster's. Even Ashley didn't scream at the funhouse mirrors, the signs that popped up, or the room set up at a slant.

When they reached the exit, all four of them squinted in the afternoon sun. The officer standing guard was the only sign of police left. When he noticed them, he turned and clenched his jaw.

"What do you think you're doing? How did you get in there?"

Kathy passed Ashley off to him. "This little girl was taken from her mother. She lives on Cherokee Drive. My sister can give you her address."

The officer took the little girl without question. Ashley wrapped her tiny fist around the collar of his shirt. The other hand played idly with the cord of his walkie talkie.

Samantha stepped forward, pushing her persuasion on the officer for the second time that day. "You're not going to remember us entering. You're only going to remember that this little girl is named Ashley and she needs to get home to her mother, Laurel Benderson. Oh, and the man who took her is in the tent. He's dead. It was self-defense on my husband's part. But the kidnapper doesn't have a background, so he won't be missed."

The officer blinked, confused by the effect of her magic and the information unloading she gave him. Finally, he nodded and said, "Yeah, uh…okay. Yeah, that makes sense."

"Make sure Ashley gets home safe," Kathy said, starting to lead them away from the tent.

The officer nodded as they walked away. "Right. I will. Thank you!"

The sisters and Steven picked up the pace until they were out of earshot of the officer.

"That's the first thank you I think we've ever gotten from someone nonmagical," Kathy muttered.

"I don't care about that right now," Samantha said. She clung to her husband's hand even as they ran to the car. "I just want to get out of here before we're stopped for more questioning."

CHAPTER 43

Sunday morning was a stark contrast from Saturday. There was a drizzle in the air that brought the temperature down and reminded Kathy that it was still technically spring and not summer, as it had felt all the previous week.

Standing outside Jeremy's door, she knocked and pulled her sweater tighter around herself.

He answered in a T-shirt and sweatpants. His hair stood on end and she was sure he had just woken up, but at least his eyes were clear. Not like Friday night.

"Hey, can I come in?" she asked. "We need to talk."

"That's never good." Still, he stood aside and let her come inside.

"Where's Michael?"

"At Maddie's," he said. "Apparently they got in a huge fight on Friday so he went over to try to patch things up."

"Hmm," Kathy said, noting the similarities between the two couples.

"So it's just me," he added. "Did you want to sit? Want anything to drink?"

"We can sit, but I'm all set with anything else."

Jeremy stepped into the living room and used the remote control to turn off the TV. He sat on the couch and moved over to make room for her. She opted for the chair.

"So?" he prompted.

She took a deep breath. *Now or never*, she told herself. "I didn't like how I was blindsided by your drinking problem the other night."

"I don't have a drinking problem."

"Clearly, you do," she pushed. "You were a mess on Friday, Jeremy. Totally embarrassing for me and you. Plus, Michael told me how you've been at the bar drunk every week for a while now."

"Oh, so you're believing Michael over me?"

"Why would he have any reason to lie?"

"Maybe because he wants to get in your pants."

Kathy rolled her eyes. "Not everything is about sex, Jeremy!" She waited for a reply and when one never came, she added, "Fine. Let's forget what Michael told me. How about the fact that *I* noticed that you have to have a drink at every meal."

"I have a right to unwind. So what? It's not like I'm hurting anybody."

"You're hurting yourself."

"So you say."

"It's more than that, though, Jeremy. You *lied* to me."

"I never lied."

"You never told me how much you were going out. Lying by omission is the same thing."

Jeremy scoffed and looked away from her.

"You told me Friday night that you were drinking because you didn't like your job. But instead of confiding in me, you drank your problems away, causing more problems for me and Michael who needed to drag your ass out of that bar."

He snapped his head around and pointed a finger at her. "I *did* tell you that I wasn't happy there. *You* blew me off!"

Kathy bit her tongue because that much was true. At least partly. She didn't intend to blow him off, but she could see how he would felt that way. Instead, she said, "We're slipping into bad habits again. Last time we stopped communicating with each other, we broke up."

Jeremy studied his hands. The most response he offered was a shrug.

"I don't want to keep repeating the same mistakes over and over again."

"So what do you want to do?" he asked.

"I think we should break up." Saying those words took a lot

for Kathy. She never thought she'd willingly walk away from Jeremy, but she had had enough. Maybe someday they could come back together again. After they'd both grown up a bit more. They had reconnected once, why couldn't they do it again?

"Obviously, neither of us are ready for this kind of commitment," she went on. "We're both changing. Going through things. I think it's for the best."

He stared at his hands, subtly nodding his head.

She waited for his response. And waited. And waited.

"Are you even going to say anything?"

"Okay."

"That's it? That's all you have to say?"

He stood, not looking in her direction, and stepped to the door. He held it open for her.

She sat where she was and looked at him. "Maybe this could just be a break. Give us both some space until we figure out where we stand with one another. Get our stuff together, you know?"

Jeremy looked out the door, then down at his feet, still without a word.

"You're really not going to say anything?" she asked, feeling her heart shatter.

Silence.

Feeling the lump in her throat, Kathy stood and started to the door. She stopped in front of him, where he finally met her eyes.

She could tell deep down inside that this was the final straw for both of them. Neither of them were happy and if they forced this relationship—now or later—they would end up exactly like the illusion she experienced in the funhouse.

Kathy gave him a sad smile and walked out. She made it to Samantha's car before she broke down.

CHAPTER 44

Kathy sat against her headboard, the application Trisha had given her resting on her legs. It was still blank. She stared out the window, watching as the setting sun cast its rays down Arlington Road.

The clicking heels from the hallway turned her attention to the doorway, where her sister stood, putting on a pair of earrings.

"Date night?" Kathy asked.

Samantha smiled. "Yeah. Steven and I are going to the same place he proposed last year. I told him it'd be my treat since he took out his first bad guy yesterday."

The younger sister laughed. "How's he doing with that?"

"At first he was freaked out that he killed something. Then

I explained that a malevolent being like that whose nature it is to harm can't be looked at the same way as a person with free will and choice can. It's more black and white with these guys. People are covered in gray areas."

"So he's doing better now?"

Samantha nodded. "Seems to be. I'm sure it's still on his mind, but so was the shapeshifter. And the valkyries. And—well, I guess that's all he's experienced firsthand."

"Wasn't the thing with the valkyries right after he found out you were a witch?"

"Right. So he didn't actually see them, but you and I disappeared for a while. Anyway, my point is, he'll get over the trickster too."

"Yeah."

"What about you?" Samantha asked. "Any big plans tonight? Or are you just going to Jeremy's?"

"No, I'm not going to Jeremy's." Kathy let out a deep breath. "We broke up."

The older sister sat on the edge of the bed. "Oh, I'm so sorry."

Emotion began to overcome Kathy again. She thought she had cried enough all day to get over the events of earlier that morning, but apparently it was still a fresh wound that needed more time to heal.

Kathy shrugged. "I'm sorry. I know you guys wanted to have the house to yourselves tonight, but I kind of just want to stay in tonight."

"No, of course." Samantha watched her sister begin to cry, then came around to Kathy's side and pulled her in for a hug. "What happened?"

"I talked to him about his drinking and how he turned to that instead of talking to me about what he was going through with his job and everything. He didn't think there was a problem. Didn't seem to have any issue with the fact that we have been down this road before." She sucked in a shuddering breath. "So I ended it."

"What did he say to that?"

She tried to swallow down the lump in her throat, but it persisted. "Just 'Okay.' Then he ignored me when I tried to talk to him more about it. He opened the door for me and made it very clear that I wasn't welcome there anymore." That was a memory she knew she wouldn't ever forget.

"Oh, Kathy." Samantha pulled her in for another hug, squeezing her tighter than the first time. "That's terrible. I'm so sorry it ended like that." She pulled away and looked at her sister. "If it makes you feel any better, you ended it for the right reasons. Couples should always be honest with each other. Even when it's difficult."

"Like you and Steven?"

"I wouldn't say we're always a model couple, but—"

"He mentioned something yesterday about the baby not being magical." This had been on Kathy's mind for a while, as well as everything with Jeremy. "Where would he get an idea like that from?"

Samantha looked down at the floor. "Yeah, I told him that. And I'm not proud of it. But…" She sighed. "It's obvious he's still not perfectly okay with me being a witch. He never says anything against it, but sometimes I wish he didn't have to deal with that part of my life."

"But that part of our lives is a *huge* part of our lives," Kathy said. "For better or worse, that's what he agreed to. Besides, he knew before you got married. He could've backed out."

"Easier said than done."

Kathy didn't budge, so Samantha went on.

"I don't know. I just thought that if he didn't have to worry about his son or daughter also being a witch that he wouldn't feel so alone. So worried. So freaked out that he's the only nonmagical person living in a house full of witches."

"Sam, he married you for a reason. He's made his decision. Yeah, there might be an adjustment period, but let him adjust to it while you're pregnant instead of building resentment toward your kid after they're born."

Samantha shook her head. "You and I haven't had a chance to talk much about the illusions the trickster put us through."

"The one where you accidentally killed Steven?"

"I had another one too."

"What did you see?"

Samantha played with the wedding ring on her finger.

"Well, Steven found out I lied to him about our baby being a witch. Then he found out and…he left me. Because the baby had magic. Said he couldn't live that life anymore."

"So that's even more reason to tell him now!"

"Don't you see, though? What if I tell him and he tells me it's over? Then I'm a divorced single mother who runs into danger all the time because I'm also a witch. What kind of life is that for a kid? What kind of mother would I be?"

"Steven's not going to leave you."

"You didn't see the illusion. It was—"

"It wasn't real!" Kathy whisper-shouted. They had been keeping their voices down, but Kathy felt her enthusiasm overcoming her so she tried to reign it in. "The trickster was trying to *scare* you. He embellished your worst fears. Everything will be fine if you tell your husband the truth. Take it from me. Don't keep any secrets from him."

"Maybe you're right," Samantha admitted. "But also, there's a chance that our baby *won't* have magic and all this will be water under the bridge."

"That's a very small chance, Sam. And it's not one you can count on, nor should you."

"Anyway, it'll be a while before our child starts to develop magic," Samantha said. "Several years, actually."

Kathy shook her head as her sister spoke. "No, no, *no*, Sam! Stop lying to him."

"It'll work out. It'll be fine."

"You don't believe that."

Samantha peered around Kathy's shoulder at the alarm clock on the bedside table. "Oh wow. It's getting late. I'm sure Steven's downstairs waiting for me."

"This conversation isn't over," Kathy said. "What you're doing isn't right and I don't support it."

"What I'm doing is within the confines of my own marriage. You might not think it's right, but it's not your business to butt in."

Kathy bit her lip and watched her sister walk out. It wasn't until she heard the front door close that she turned back to what she had been working on before her sister entered.

This was a turning point for everyone, but especially Kathy. Even though dropping out of college had been a snap decision, it was one that she didn't regret. It was the right choice because she hadn't been happy there.

As she turned her attention to the application for the receptionist position, Kathy felt that this was the right move for her. She felt like she was stepping up in the world. This change would be a good one.

CHAPTER 45

The restaurant hadn't changed much since they'd been there last. Almost a year ago. Back then, Samantha had just graduated college, was worried about finding a job, and was unexpectedly getting engaged. Since then, she'd secured her job, gotten married, become financially stable, and she was now pregnant. It felt almost full circle and she wondered what her life would be like in another year's time.

"Maybe we should make this dinner an annual thing," she suggested. "Use it as a milestone marker to appreciate everything we've done."

"It hasn't quite been a year since I proposed here," he said. "We still have another month."

"Still. Our lives have changed dramatically."

"For the better."

"Of course."

Steven reached for his water glass. He had opted not to have any alcohol because Samantha couldn't have any. Not that they drank all too often. But on a date night like this, a glass of wine or champagne wasn't uncommon.

"I'd like to make a toast to you."

Samantha rolled her eyes with a smile. "Stop it."

"You're looking exceptionally beautiful tonight," he went on. His own goofy grin was all over his face. "And you're glowing, thanks to the help of our child. I love you, Samantha."

She humored him by lifting her own water glass and clinking it with his before taking a sip. "I love you too, but enough with the praise. Let's just enjoy a nice, peaceful dinner. I'm considering this a celebration that I'm moving on to the next trimester. Plus, we need to soak up these outings as much as possible. Once the baby comes, things will be completely different."

"In all seriousness, I just want you to know how much I appreciate you."

"Steven, please." Samantha tried to push aside the gratitude. After the conversation she had had with Kathy before she left, she didn't think she deserved it. What kind of wife lies to her husband about their child?

"Just hear me out," he insisted. "I know you've kind of been feeling down about yourself lately, but I do appreciate everything you're doing for us. For our family."

"Well, I'm just sorry that another…*magical* emergency had to interrupt our long weekend. And that you needed to…" Her voice trailed off and she gave a look around to all the people in the restaurant.

He chuckled and reached for the bread basket that had been set between them. "I never thought I'd have to drive a wooden stake through someone's heart before, but when I saw you were cornered I didn't even hesitate."

"Are you sure you're doing okay, though?" she asked. "I mean, that was a big thing to do."

He shook his head. "I'd do it again in a heartbeat if you were in danger like that. I can't imagine doing life with anyone else but you. You're a great wife, you're going to be a great mother, and that's all that truly matters."

Samantha sat back with a big smile on her face and tears in her eyes. Steven certainly loved her. And he thought a lot about her. She only hoped she could continue to live up to his standards.

You never know what will follow you home.

While touring a fixer-upper they're considering buying, Samantha and Steven both have bad feelings about the house. Samantha, who is seven months pregnant, feels a wave of energy come over her as Steven and the realtor go down to the look at the basement without her. Deciding to pass on the abandoned house, Samantha and Steven later return home without a second thought about the house.

Meanwhile, Kathy has been busy planning Samantha's baby shower with Steven's mother. It's not until Steven points out Samantha's odd behavior that Kathy begins to notice it too. As the baby shower looms nearer, Kathy is determined to figure out what's going on with her sister before Samantha is the center of attention in front of everyone.

When Kathy and Steven consult a medium about what might be going on, they learn that Samantha is very likely possessed by a poltergeist. And with her growing baby in her belly, the evil spirit may prove impossible to exorcise.

Poltergeist is the ninth book in the Coven series, which serves as a prequel to the Under the Moon series.

POLTERGEIST

COVEN: BOOK 9

Read on for an excerpt of the next book in
the Coven series!

DAVID NETH

CHAPTER 1

- OCTOBER 1934 -

Henry Powell sat on a bench at the playground in Gridley Park across from his school. The crunchy leaves blew across the grass as passersby tucked their hands deeper into their coats against the chilly breeze.

The joy of that after school feeling was lost on Henry. He had been given strict instructions to come right home after school let out, but still he lingered. As he watched groups of other kids, he swung his feet on the bench and thought about how he would rather be anywhere but home.

He wasn't welcome there.

He didn't want to stay in school, either. Many of the friends he had started grammar school with had left to go work for their families. Henry had only managed to stay in school because his grandfather had left them their house when he died, and it was fully paid for since he was the one who had built it. No need for Henry to work to bring money home for the family. At least, that's what his mother argued whenever his father tried to bring up the topic.

After several minutes of sitting on the park bench, he decided he couldn't put off going home any longer. If it got much later, his father would be waiting and would know that he didn't come right home. With a deep sigh, he got to his feet and proceeded down the street toward home.

When Henry finally made it back, he sat on the front steps of his house. Even before he entered, he could hear his parents arguing inside.

"…you let the kid do whatever he wants!" his father shouted. "He needs to learn discipline!"

"He needs to be a kid!" his mother shouted back. "What are you doing? That's my mother's—*Ivan!*"

Glass shattered.

"Do you know how much that cost?" she asked. "It's irreplaceable!"

"Go make your kid work like everyone else's kids and maybe then we can afford to buy another!"

"You only broke it because it was mine! What if I had poured your booze down the drain? Or broken your rocker?"

"You wouldn't dare!"

Henry could hear the distinct sounds of his father hitting

his mother. Of her collapsing to the floor. The silence was worse than the arguing. At least if they were arguing, he wasn't hitting her. Not usually, at least.

Rising to his feet, Henry rushed inside. Sure enough, his mother lay on the floor, cradling her cheek while his father stood over her, watching her struggle.

"And where the hell have you been, boy?" his father asked him. "School let out half an hour ago! Did that stupid little head of yours get lost?"

"No," Henry said quietly.

"Then what took you so long?" Suddenly, Henry was face-to-face with the full force of his father's rage. He had been here before—several times, actually.

Henry stammered. He wanted to tell his father to go away. To leave him and his mother alone and never talk to them again. But he couldn't. His father wasn't going anywhere. And even if he did, there was no way they could survive. His father was the only one who worked in the household. He brought home the money that they used to go to the market. He paid the bills that kept them in their house. He earned enough so that Henry didn't have to go to work himself.

Before Henry could respond to his father, his mother stepped in between them, putting her son behind her.

"Leave him alone," she said. "Let the boy have some peace and quiet in this house for once in his life!"

Henry watched as his father studied the two of them. There

wasn't a trace of love in his eyes. Only obligation. He was stuck with these people and he certainly wasn't happy about it. Henry felt the same way about him.

Finally, he turned and stalked off to the front door. "I'm going to the bar."

Both mother and son watched as he left. Neither of them dared move until he was out of sight.

"Are you okay?" Henry asked his mother.

She waved it off. "Nothing that some ice can't fix." She dropped to her knees and took his face in her hands, offering a sad smile even as she winced at the pain. "What about you, sweetie? How are you? How was your day?"

Henry shrugged. "When's he coming back?"

His mother shook her head. "I don't know, dear. Probably not for a while, which means it's you and me for dinner. I was thinking about making spaghetti. I know it's your favorite. What do you think about that?"

Henry's mind was still on his father. He cast a look toward the front door and said, "I'm scared."

His mother's face drooped to a frown as she pulled him in for a tight hug. "I know, honey. But I'll always protect you. Remember that."

Henry smiled and kissed his mother on the cheek—the side that wasn't rapidly swelling.

"What do you say after dinner we listen to some music and relax in the living room before bed?" she suggested. "Just the two of us. We'll have fun together."

Henry nodded and grinned for his mother's benefit. "Okay."

As his mother went into the kitchen to fix their food, Henry stood in picture window and hoped that his father would stay gone. It was a hope he knew would never come.

CHAPTER 2

- OCTOBER 1989 -

Kathy checked her watch as she waited for her second bus to arrive. She had just gotten out of work and was meeting Steven's mother at her house to finalize plans for Samantha's baby shower in two days.

Tucking her hands deeper into her pockets, Kathy braced herself against the wind. It was almost the end of October so the weather had turned. She hadn't noticed how cold it had gotten because she had been in the warm office all day.

Dr. Newberg had hired her to take over for Trisha as a receptionist back in June. So far she enjoyed having the steady paycheck and a reason to leave the house each day that didn't result in even more work needing to be done when she came home. But, she could already feel that the nine-to-five routine was weighing on her.

The second bus arrived and Kathy stepped on, dropping her fare in before taking her seat. She sat near the front. The bus ride wouldn't be long—if the weather wasn't so cold, she would've just walked the rest of the way after getting off at the first stop. As it was, her newfound financial security allowed her to take an extra bus ride if it meant staying warmer for a few more minutes.

By time Kathy arrived at Mary's house, she had already braced herself for overly friendly smiles, subtle jabs, and an argumentative tone. She knew the drill because they had met a couple times already. Just like Samantha and Steven's wedding earlier that year, Mary wanted to have a huge elegant party. Kathy knew her sister would only want something small and intimate, possibly even at someone's house.

"Kathy! Hello dear! Come on in." Mary waved her in with a smile. Kathy was grateful to get out of the damp, chilly air.

"How've you been?" Kathy pulled off her coat and added it to the closet by the door.

"Just lovely, dear," she said quickly before jumping right into her first crisis of the meeting. "I've been thinking about the schedule we've committed to for Saturday." She led Kathy inside with an arm around her. At the table, there were already papers and invitations and menus that the two of them had gone over extensively during previous visits.

"Did the caterers confirm?"

"Oh yes, that's all taken care of." Mary took a seat at the table and reached for her reading glasses. "And we've already had everyone RSVP, so we'll have a full house at the golf club."

The shower was going to be at the Lawrence Park Golf Club, since Mary's brother was a member and was able to get them the reservation for a discount. The cost was still kind of steep for Kathy's budget, but she agreed in order to appease Mary. Sometimes it was better to do that than to waste the energy arguing your point.

"So what's the issue then?" Kathy took the seat beside her.

"Well, with the brunch, the opening of the gifts, and taking pictures, I'm not sure how many of these games of yours we'll be able to get to."

"You're saying you don't think we'll be able to do them at all?" Kathy had already narrowed down the list of games to only three. And she tried to only list ones that would fit in with Mary's standards. Oh, and something that Samantha would enjoy. Funny how through all of this planning, the person they were celebrating sometimes had been forgotten.

Mary rocked her head back and forth, studying the schedule in front of her. "We'll have to see if there's time."

"I'd like to make time for them."

She chuckled. "Oh honey, you can't *schedule* fun."

"Well, we need to give our guests something to *do*," Kathy said. "I'm sure Sam isn't going to want everyone gawking at her all day."

Mary rolled her eyes. "Yes, I'm well aware of her stance on people touching her belly."

Kathy decided to let it slide. That had been a whole separate argument between Samantha and Mary, who thought it was appropriate to rub Samantha's stomach without warning whenever they saw each other.

"I think the games will be the perfect distraction so that Samantha doesn't have to swat away hands the whole time," Kathy said. "We're doing this for her. I want her to enjoy it."

Mary huffed. "Well okay then. I suppose we can cut the photos a little short, but that still only gives us twenty minutes."

Kathy took the schedule from Mary and reached for a nearby pen. "Okay. Well, we can get rid of dessert time. We can just serve them at the same time as the rest of brunch and let people take what they want. That'll save us another half an hour, which leaves almost a full hour for the games." She passed it back to Mary, who looked under her glasses at it.

"Yes, well, I suppose that could work. But you're going to have to call the caterer to tell them about the change!"

"Not a problem. I think it'll be a lot of fun!"

"Oh, I do too," Mary said with the first genuine smile Kathy had seen that day. "I just hope that everyone dresses appropriately. Make sure you wear something nice, dear. Do you have anything that'll work?"

Biting her tongue, Kathy said, "Yes, I have several options to choose from."

Mary looked her up and down. "You have been dressing more grown-up lately."

"I'm working at a doctor's office now."

"That's right. I think Samantha mentioned that the last time we all had dinner. You dropped out of college for it?"

Kathy flashed a smile in an effort to hold in her anger at her sister. "Not for this job, no. But yes, I'm no longer in school."

Samantha hadn't been happy that Kathy had dropped out of college. Kathy thought that blow would be softened by the fact that she had a job at the doctor's office lined up, but Samantha still wanted her sister to follow "the plan." Kathy didn't think that Samantha would take their disagreement out to other people, though. Least of all, Mary.

"Anyway," Mary said, "I think it'll be a splendid day. A nice, formal event that we can remember fondly later."

"Not too formal," Kathy reminded her.

"Yes, yes. I remember their wedding at the *fire hall*." She made a face. "And thank you for asking me to plan it with you, dear. I've very much enjoyed being a part of it."

Kathy had only asked her because Steven thought it would be nice to include his mother. And Kathy didn't disagree, but working with Mary took patience. She was just grateful that the baby shower was almost here and gone so that she could be done working so closely with Mary.

"You're very welcome," Kathy said with a smile. "Is there anything else you wanted to discuss?

"I think we've thought of everything," Mary said. "Remember to call the caterer and notify them of the change with the desserts."

"Yes, I will." Looking again at her watch, Kathy rose to her feet. "I have to get going. I have a date."

"Oh? Will we be planning another baby shower soon? After the wedding, of course."

Kathy laughed nervously. "Not exactly. This is just the first date. I've only met the guy once. So we'll see how tonight goes."

"Just remember not to do anything stupid, dear."

CHAPTER 3

The house smelled musty and dank. Like an old garage. Every floorboard creaked, except the ones that had rotted through. There were some beautiful leaded windows on the first floor, but many other windows had been boarded up throughout the years. In several corners there were piles of leaves and garbage, indicating that the house hadn't been completely sealed from critters and squatters.

"This is..." Samantha paused, one hand on her belly as she looked around and searched for the word to use.

"It needs a lot of work," Steven said pointedly.

"Well yes," their realtor, Rupert, said with a nod of his head. "But you said you were looking for a fixer-upper."

"I guess I just didn't realize it would need this

much…um…*fixing-up*." Samantha was still in awe at how dilapidated this house was. It looked beautiful outside. A little rough, but nothing that they couldn't handle. Inside was…well, it was too much for them.

"Just keep an open mind and look around," Rupert said. "There are three bedrooms upstairs, a full bath upstairs as well." He pointed toward the back of the house. "The previous owners started to put in a half bath off the kitchen, but I think they got in over their head with renovations and stopped part of the way through."

"How long ago was that?" Steven asked. "It looks like it's been sitting empty for a while."

Again, Rupert nodded. "It's been vacant for a long time, yes. *But!* Think of this as your opportunity to bring life back to this house. You know, this used to be a family home. Back when this was built, these houses held generations of families. Think of the holidays and celebrations and the *life* that happened here. I'd hate to see all of that history wasted if it ends up on the city's demolition list."

Samantha nodded. He had a point, even if she could see right through his sales pitch. She had agreed to look at older homes with character and history because that's what she loved about her own house. With the baby coming, she was convinced that she and Steven needed their own place. And maybe borrowing someone else's history wouldn't be so bad. Maybe she could learn to love an old house that hadn't always belonged to her family.

"Think about it," Rupert went on. "You could finish off the bathroom down here. The hardwoods would look nice once you refinished them."

"And replaced a few," Steven added.

Rupert nodded. "And the light reflecting through these windows would be breathtaking, especially on a Sunday morning when you're sipping your coffee on the couch, watching the leaves change on the gorgeous mature trees along the street. And Gridley Park is just around the corner. This really is a very nice neighborhood. I'm sure you'll get to know all the neighbors in no time!"

Steven leaned toward Samantha and said, "He's really trying to sell us on this place."

She smirked back. "What do you think?"

"I think it'd take a lot of work, but we could do it," he said. "We'd have to fix the floors, work on any structural issues with the foundation, check the roof, that kind of stuff. After that we can do the pretty stuff."

"And we're going to do all of this in two months before the baby's born?"

Rupert scoffed, but offered nothing else. He stepped to the front window and looked out, pretending not to listen.

"If we decide to buy it, the sale of this house wouldn't even go through before the baby comes," Steven explained. "This would have to be over the next year."

Samantha looked around. She tried to imagine spending

the next year working on a house while also taking care of a newborn. Oh, and maintaining her full-time job and her duties as a witch.

But it was more than that. Despite it's history and neighborhood location—both things she had wanted in the search for a new house—the house gave Samantha a bad feeling. Like something bad had happened here. She wasn't sure if that was the current state of the house, her pregnancy, or her witch intuition warning her to leave, but the whole place was sending out bad vibes.

"You don't seem like you like it," Steven said.

"Keep in mind that it's dreary out today," Rupert butt in. "When it's the summer time and the sun's shining full force, this place will look great!"

"Do you mind if we have a minute to discuss?" Steven asked.

"No, that's okay," Samantha said. "Let's see the rest of the house. We can talk about it more at home."

Rupert waited until Steven turned to him, as if signaling to go ahead.

"All right then," he said with a smile. "Let's head upstairs and look at the bedrooms!"

The upstairs was small. The ceilings were low—although Rupert suggested they vaulted them to give them more headspace. The bedrooms were also small. The "master" was only slightly bigger than the two other rooms and the bathroom left much to be desired. Tile pieces were falling off the walls. The floors were rotting from dripping water lines before they had been disconnected by the city. Not to mention the fact that there was only a tub and an outdated toilet that likely wouldn't meet modern code enforcement standards. Samantha was just grateful that squatters or critters didn't leave any excrement "surprises."

Back downstairs, Rupert led them to the kitchen.

"Now, you might want to consider taking this wall down between these two rooms," he suggested. "I'm not sure if it's structural so you'd have to have that checked out before you did anything, but wouldn't it look nice to have everything open? And all the natural light would just flood in from all the windows! Remember, many of them are still boarded up."

Samantha was only half listening. Her attention was on the basement door. It made her uneasy. Some sort of negative energy radiated from there and she wanted to get as far away as possible.

"Right here we have the half bath I told you about before." Rupert indicated a small room off the back porch addition. "You can really customize that however you want. It's a clean slate!"

"This kitchen actually doesn't look half bad," Steven commented. "It's pretty big, which I guess is nice because we'd have to put a dining table in here too."

Rupert nodded. "Just update the appliances, give everything a good cleaning and a coat of paint, and you should be all set."

Even Samantha had to agree that the kitchen was in decent shape. She could almost smell the home-cooked meals that had once been prepared here. As she looked around at the cabinets, her eyes kept flickering back to the basement.

What happened down there? she wondered.

"So the utilities have been cut off by the city?" Steven asked.

Rupert nodded. "Yes, so the house hasn't been winterized in…a while."

"Do you mind if I take a look and see what kind of damage there is?"

"Steven!" Samantha blurted as he made a move toward the basement door.

Both men looked at her with confused looks.

"What's the matter?" he asked.

She looked between the two of them. Steven would understand her concerns—or at least respect them. She was too embarrassed to share her fears in front of Rupert as well.

"Nothing," she muttered. "Just…be careful. You don't know what's down there."

He pulled a flashlight from his jacket pocket and clicked it on. "I'll keep an eye out. Don't worry. You should stay up here, though. I don't want you breathing in any fumes or anything that might be trapped down there."

I wouldn't dream of going down there, she thought to herself, but simply nodded.

When the two men disappeared down the stairs, Samantha

suddenly felt isolated. She heard scratching coming from somewhere. She turned to try to follow the noise, but the more she moved, the more the sound seemed to drift to somewhere new.

It's fine. You're fine. Just relax. It's an old house. There are probably squirrels living in the walls.

Turning to the kitchen cabinets, she idly opened up each one. They were all empty, some still smelling of cinnamon or olive oil or basil. The cabinet on the end, however, had several recipes taped on the inside of the cabinet door.

"Edith's meatloaf."

"Cindy's pecan pie."

"Martha's sauce."

Samantha smiled. This was the kind of history she wanted in an old house. Even though it wasn't hers, she liked the idea of living somewhere that had been a family home before. Somewhere that had been filled with love and life, only to experience it all again with Samantha's own family. She still preferred that to be the house she grew up in, but unless Kathy moved out—and Samantha wasn't about to kick her out of her own house—then she and Steven needed to get their own place. That's what it ultimately came down to.

Samantha noticed something at the back of the cabinet. Stretching up to her tiptoes, she reached for it and pulled it toward her.

A family stared back at her. Three people posed for the

photograph. The father had a stern brow and a mean look. The mother had a tense smile. And the little boy just looked sad.

This was the type of thing that Samantha would ordinarily love to have in an old house, but it just gave her the chills. Why did these people look so miserable? Was this the family that had lived here? What actually happened in this house?

Suddenly, a rush of wind hit Samantha out of nowhere. She dropped the frame to the floor as the gust pushed her back several feet.

And just as quickly as it came, it was gone.

"Sam!" Steven called from the basement. "You okay?"

She didn't respond, too shaken by what had happened. It felt like something supernatural, but she didn't feel any different. Had she just imagined it?

"Sam!" Steven called again when he made it to the top of the stairs. Rupert wasn't far behind. "What happened?"

"I—I tripped," she stammered. "Dropped the frame."

Rupert stepped up and picked up the photograph. He turned it upside down to let the broken glass fall to the floor, then used his foot to brush it against the base of the lower cabinets.

"Hmm," he said. "I wonder if this is the family that lived here."

"That's what I thought too," she said.

Steven eyed her another moment, then turned to look at the picture. "That's kind of neat."

"So!" Samantha said, a little louder than she had intended. "How's everything look downstairs?"

"Old," Steven said. "Outdated. Everything probably needs to be replaced."

"Sounds expensive," she said.

"I'm sorry, Rupert." He stepped to the basement door to close it. "We're going to have to look at our budget and—what's this?" He pointed to the back of the basement door.

Rupert walked up and examined it with him.

"There's scratches," Steven said.

Samantha remained glued to the floor where she was. There was no way she was going anywhere near that basement. All she wanted to do was leave.

"Yes, it appears that way," Rupert said.

"There are full-on *gouges* in the door!"

"Perhaps it was from a dog locked in the basement," he said. "Or an animal got in since it's been abandoned. A basement door like that? That's a simple replacement."

"Everything just keeps adding up in this house, though," Steven muttered as he closed the door. "This is going to cost a small fortune to get up to snuff."

"Yes, well, I suppose that's something to consider," Rupert murmured. Then, more jovially, "Anyway, what do you think? Now that you've seen the whole house?"

Husband and wife looked at each other. Finally, Samantha shook her head.

"I don't like it," she said. "It makes me feel uncomfortable."

Steven nodded. "It's a big job and I would love to see it restored, but I don't think we're the ones to do it."

Rupert sighed heavily. "Well, that's fair enough."

"Thank you for your time," Steven added. "Maybe you can find us another house that doesn't need so much work."

The realtor led them to the door, his spirit clearly deflated. "I'll see what I can do. In the meantime, if you spot any houses you'd like to look at, just give me a call and I'll set it up for you."

They bid their goodbyes to Rupert and climbed into their car. The whole way home, Samantha still felt the chill from the house deep in her bones.

FIND ALL THE BOOKS IN THE COVEN SERIES!

MORE BY THE AUTHOR

To find more books by the author, visit
DavidNethBooks.com/Books

* * *

Subscribe to his newsletter to be the first to know of new
releases and special deals!
DavidNethBooks.com/Newsletter

* * *

**If you enjoyed the book, please consider leaving a
review on Goodreads or the retailer you bought it from.**
Reviews help potential readers determine whether
they'll enjoy a book, so any comments on what you
thought of the story would be very helpful!

About the Author

David Neth is the author of the Coven series, the Under the Moon series, Heat series, the Fuse series, and other stories. He lives in Batavia, NY, where he dreams of a successful publishing career and opening his own bookstore.

Also writes small town romance as D. Allen.

www.DavidNethBooks.com

www.facebook.com/DavidNethBooks